A Vineyard Blizzard

The Vineyard Sunset Series

Katie Winters

ALL RIGHTS RESERVED. No part of this publication may be
reproduced, distributed, or transmitted in any form or by any means,
including photocopying, recording, or other electronic or mechanical
methods, without the prior written permission of the publisher.

Copyright © 2022 by Katie Winters

This is a work of fiction. Any resemblance of characters to actual persons,
living or dead is purely coincidental. Katie Winters holds exclusive rights
to this work. Unauthorized duplication is prohibited.

Chapter One

The little rose-colored house in East Boston was hardly big enough for any sort of get-together, let alone a wake, especially for Evelyn Ellis, who had been widely known as "the socialite of Eastie" prior to her death. As mourners gathered over clam chowder, buttery rolls, pies, and casseroles, they spoke of Evelyn's soft yet confident nature, the parties she'd arranged, and the birthday cards she'd sent.

"Nobody could play the clarinet like she could," a community band member affirmed, his brow furrowed as he held a bright orange carrot stick aloft.

"And that's not to mention her life before Boston," a gray-haired woman chimed in, turning her eyes directly toward Lola Sheridan, who stood off to the side in a black turtleneck dress and a pair of heeled black boots.

"She met that Italian man," the woman beside her whispered discreetly, "during her journey across Rome and Tuscany."

"Nobody was better looking than Evelyn back in the

1

day," the first woman stated. "She could have had any man she pleased."

"But instead, she dragged that Gasbarro Italian back to the United States, didn't she?"

"She sure did."

Lola caught sight of Tommy Gasbarro through the farther doorframe, where he'd been corraled in conversation by his mother's pastor. She grinned to herself as love shimmered through her heart and across her stomach. Tommy, who'd always been a loner, looked slightly pained at the nonstop conversation, yet his love for his mother kept him there, holding down the fort after her sudden absence.

"Evelyn talked about how he hardly learned a single word of English before he left her and went back to Rome," another woman quipped. "And that was all before she met Stan Ellis."

"Goodness me. How many times was she married?"

"Just the once," the first woman replied. She seemed to be an authority on Evelyn Ellis. "She kept Stan's last name because she loved him more than her daddy, so she didn't want to go back to his name. In fact, I thought I saw Stan somewhere around here."

Lola's throat tightened at the mention of Stan. Although she and the rest of the Sheridan clan had made their peace with Stan Ellis and his affair with Anna Sheridan, his mistake had resulted in Anna's death. This was to be a forever jagged scar on Lola's heart.

When Tommy had first learned the news of his mother's stroke and subsequent death, he'd sat at the edge of the bed he and Lola shared and stared at his feet for fifteen full minutes, wordless. Lola had sat beside him, her hand over his, waiting. There hadn't been anything to say. The first thing he'd finally managed to say was, "I had better call Stan."

Although Tommy had offered to drive Stan up to the funeral from Martha's Vineyard, Stan had insisted on driving himself. Lola had spotted him in the back row of the funeral home with his head bowed throughout the ceremony. As far as Lola knew, Stan had loved two women in his life: her mother and Evelyn. Now, they were both gone. That must have felt very strange indeed for Stan. Now there were whispers about his affection for Nancy Remington, the widow who operated the Katama Lodge and Wellness Spa on the southeastern tip of Martha's Vineyard. Still, Lola couldn't give weight to this gossip. She did know that Stan had been instrumental in saving Nancy's life as last autumn's Hurricane Janine had threatened to ransack the island.

"If you'll excuse me." Lola stepped around the ladies at the food table to restock the drinks, grab more paper napkins and plates, and fetch another bag of ice from Evelyn's garage. Being "in charge" like this wasn't the typical Lola way. As she hustled, she channeled her elder sister, Susan, who always knew what to do, how to do it, and what to say to make everyone feel better. Lola, the more hotheaded and free-spirited sister, had never been a homemaker, per se. For years, she'd raised her daughter, Audrey, on a piddling journalist's salary, resisted serious romantic relationships, and called herself "anti-family."

Oh, how things changed.

A sturdy hand caught her elbow. She stalled, taking a step back, finding Tommy's dark eyes peering down at her. God, he was handsome. Every bit of his Italian roots seeped through his genes, making no room for his mother's Scottish heritage. His black hair swooped over his ears, still growing thick despite his age inching toward fifty.

"You're working too hard," Tommy told her softly.

Lola stepped into him and placed her cheek against his chest. There was the thumping of his heart, assuring her that all was okay. Something about death, the reminder that everything you'd ever known would one day be gone, that terrified Lola. She told herself to appreciate the here and now— to love the current season.

"I've heard some fun stories about your mother," Lola began, lifting her chin.

"That's what Mom would have wanted. Lots of gossip at her funeral about all the chaos she caused."

Lola laughed. "I wish I would have known her better."

"Maybe it's for the best," Tommy replied sadly. "Had the two of you gotten together more often, you would have figured out you could take over the world. We'd all be doomed."

A couple of minutes later, Stan appeared before them to announce that he wanted to drive back to the Vineyard that night. His eyes were rimmed red and glassy. He shook Tommy's hand and knelt to hug Lola gently. He seemed like a defeated old man overrun by time. It was a sad vision.

"I'll call you in the new year," Tommy told Stan.

"That's right," Stan muttered. "Tomorrow's New Year's Eve. Are you two staying around Boston for a couple of days? Or heading back?"

Lola's stomach twisted. It was rare that the Sheridan

family couldn't find a reason to celebrate all together, and this New Year's Eve was no different. They'd been pretty good about occasionally inviting Stan to their holiday functions, but it wasn't always a necessity, and it wasn't always a welcome idea.

"I, for one, have a big night scheduled with my armchair," Stan told them before she could decide on an invitation. "Nancy's pestering me about coming to the Lodge, but I can't bear it. They serve too much vegan food for my liking."

Lola and Tommy chuckled good-naturedly and wished Stan a safe drive back. He pulled a thick wool hat over his ears and saluted them before weaving his way through the crowd and exiting the little rose-colored house. What a strange thing, Lola thought, to come to your ex-wife's funeral, heavy with memories from your long-ago time together.

Tommy and Lola forced their way through the next several hours. Mourners seemed awash with juicy stories about Evelyn Ellis and compliments for the ever-handsome Tommy Gasbarro.

"You really do look just like your father, that conniving Italian," one woman said. "When was the last time you saw him?"

"I was maybe four or five," Tommy told her. "But I'm told he was a very good sailor, which is how I've made my living. So I suppose I have him to thank for that in some way."

The mourners' interest in Lola was paramount.

"Tommy has never brought a girl home," a dear friend of Evelyn's informed her under her breath. "Evelyn felt he wasn't the settling down type."

"Neither of us really is," Lola told her. "Maybe that's why it works."

The woman's color drained from her cheeks. It seemed to her that not settling down went so far against the norm that it threatened society itself.

"Well, marry or don't marry," the woman returned stiffly. "But God knows the truth of what you've done."

At this, Lola and Tommy found one another's gaze and stifled laughter. The woman muttered to herself and made her way back to the snack table, where she seemed to fall into a round of gossip with another older lady. Lola sensed they spoke only about Tommy, Lola, and the downfall of marriage.

The mourners left Evelyn Ellis's home by eight o'clock that evening, leaving piles of paper plates, wadded-up napkins, light stains on the gray couch, and wine blotches on the counters in their wake. Lola stretched her arms over her head until they cracked. How did Susan host so many parties? Did she have some sort of energy reserve that Lola didn't? She was nearly six years older and had just survived a bout of cancer, for crying out loud.

Tommy disappeared into the kitchen and returned with two glasses of wine and a stack of crackers and cheese. Together, they sat on the living room floor with their backs leaned up against the gray couch. The smell of older women's perfume lingered in the air and made it difficult to breathe. Eventually, Tommy rose to crack open a window, which brought a sharp-edged breeze from the December 30th night.

"She was so loved, Tommy," Lola breathed as he rejoined her on the floor.

Tommy was stoic. He placed a cracker on his tongue

and chewed slowly. "She wasn't that old. She was only seventy-one and deserved more time. She had such a zest for life. She would have used that time better than most."

Lola's throat tightened with sorrow. There was nothing to be done about the stupidity of death.

Beautiful modern art paintings decorated the living room—things indicative of a woman who had studied art, poetry, and literature and had grand thoughts and arguments about them. A small television in the corner reflected the image of Lola and Tommy with their legs stretched out on the floor.

"I used to take her sailing," Tommy admitted softly. "I knew she was terrified of the water because she'd nearly drowned as a little girl, and the fear had never gone away. But instead of allowing that fear to take hold of her, she'd lean out over the side of the boat so far that I thought she would fall in. And she'd close her eyes and lift her chin as the wind swept over her. She looked like a painting. Always after, she'd drink a glass of wine on the dock and gaze out at the water and say something in Italian. *'Tra il dire e il fare c'e di mezzo il mare.'*"

"What does it mean?" Lola breathed.

"Between saying and doing is half a sea," Tommy explained. "A proverb that says that people so often say they'll do something and never do it. I always assumed it meant that my father had said he'd do a lot of things for her and never did. But actually, she told me later that it was more something she wanted to tell herself. She always wanted to do more than she said she would and always wanted to uphold her word."

Lola felt terribly quiet. She sipped her wine and considered this, the doing and the saying, the Italian words Evelyn had once learned and kept near her heart, despite her Italian boyfriend's abandonment.

After a little while, Tommy turned on the television. The sound of other people's voices talking about something besides death was comforting. Lola headed into the guest bedroom and removed her black dress, exchanging it for a pair of pajama pants and a lacy tank top. Tommy joined her, stripped to his boxers, then followed her back into the living room. It felt strange to be in Evelyn's house without her, as though she would soon pop out of the kitchen and ask if anyone was hungry.

"It's a bit overwhelming," Tommy admitted, dropping back onto the couch. "All the stuff I'll have to take care of over the next few months. Top priority will be clearing out this house and looking at her will."

"I'll help you with anything you need," Lola told him gently.

Tommy's dark eyes widened. "You don't have to do anything."

"Don't be silly. We're a team," Lola said, almost expecting Tommy to protest, to tell her that he wasn't the sort of man who needed a teammate. To her surprise, he didn't.

Lola cuddled against Tommy as the two settled deeper onto the couch, lost in their own thoughts. Over the previous year and a half since Lola had met Tommy and gotten involved with him after a fateful sailing expedition, Lola and Tommy had created a densely textured, often romantic, and ever-fruitful relationship, one with more nuance and love than many marriages. When Susan (and many others) questioned Lola about whether she wanted to "finally" get married, Lola always shrugged it off. She and Tommy simply weren't the marrying type.

They were extremely content with what they had, which was just fine with her.

"I love you," Tommy whispered before gently kissing the top of her head. "I hope you know how much."

Lola's heart swelled. "I love you, too— more than words."

Chapter Two

"'**B**itter Sweet Symphony.' The Verve. 1997."
Tommy snapped his fingers excitedly before
he cranked the volume on his truck radio. The
'90s tune roared through the speakers while Lola laughed,
her stomach tightening as memories coursed through her.

"You're good at this," Lola said with a crooked grin.
"I'm not used to such a worthy opponent."

"You want an expert on '80s and '90s music? You're
looking at him," Tommy replied as he turned his thumb
toward his chest. "When I hit eighteen, I skipped town to
sail full-time, usually sleeping in ports across the Atlantic
with only a radio to keep me company." Tommy then
imitated a radio announcer's voice as he said, *"This is
104.1 WWUS, your one-stop shop for all the hits here in
the Florida Keys. Or this is 93.5 – The Island! We play all
the best tracks here in Savannah, Georgia. Or, my favorite,
100.3, Classic Rock straight out of Bar Harbor, Maine."*

She turned to look at him, a wide smile plastered on
her face. "How many radio jingles do you have
memorized?"

"You don't want to know," Tommy told her. "But you can tell the true strength of a nomad by the number of radio stations he has memorized."

"Is that an ancient nomadic proverb?" Lola teased.

They'd left the rose-colored house in East Boston twenty minutes before and now sped toward Woods Hole, where they'd take the midafternoon ferry back to Oak Bluffs and join the Sheridan clan for New Year's Eve. Tommy and Lola rejoined hands in the center of the truck as The Verve's transcendent tune continued.

They sang joyfully together— Lola at forty and Tommy at forty-six, yet both remembering their vibrant teenage selves.

"I wish I could have known you in the '90s," Lola said thoughtfully as the song continued.

"I was no good for anyone," Tommy told her. "Angry with the world. Angry with myself. Eager to run away from any situation, if only because standing still made me think about how much I didn't like myself..."

Lola's throat tightened. Since she and Tommy had gotten together, Tommy had spent more time on Martha's Vineyard than any other location, something that had surprised them both. Even still, he'd been off on sailing expeditions more times than Lola had genuinely liked, even flirting with hurricane season in a way that seemed nearly suicidal. Every time Tommy darkened their cabin door again, Lola sighed with relief and gratitude. She wasn't the sort of woman to ask him to stay; he wasn't the sort of man to listen to that kind of talk, anyway.

Lola clapped with excitement during the next song as Tommy stuttered, trying to guess the title and artist.

"Okay, it's obviously called 'Damn! I Wish I Was

Your Lover,'" Tommy began, his cheeks reddening with embarrassment.

"Tell me something I don't know," Lola joked. "She only says it like eighteen thousand times throughout the song. If you really want to impress me, tell me the singer's name."

"Ugh," Tommy groaned. "I don't know."

Lola laughed vibrantly, tossing her head back. "The master has fallen!"

Tommy grabbed her hand again, brought her palm to his lips, and kissed the soft skin of her hand delicately. Lola was so surprised at the beautiful gesture that she stopped laughing abruptly, even as Sophie B. Hawkins continued to sing the beautiful, heart-wrenching song.

"What was that for?" Lola asked softly.

Tommy adjusted their hands again between the two front seats and shrugged. "Just felt like it."

"Were you overwhelmed by the emotion of Sophie B. Hawkins's beautiful lyrics?"

"That's right! Sophie B. Hawkins," Tommy said, disgruntled. "I knew it."

"Clearly, you didn't," Lola returned. "Point goes to me."

After Tommy parked the truck in the belly of the ferry, the two lovebirds leaped out and headed for the deck, where they peered through the sharp wind and sipped piping-hot coffee from the coffee cart. Ordinarily, they might have stayed below deck, shielded from the wind, but something about the last day of the year demanded you stand out in it and experience every last minute of sun. Captain Joshua greeted Lola and Tommy warmly, shaking their hands and wishing them a Happy New Year.

"Good to see you around these parts so late in the year, Tommy. You're normally off on some beach by October or November, letting the rest of us here freeze to death," Joshua joked. He then gave Lola a warm smile and added, "You've really confused him, haven't you?"

"Now listen here," Tommy returned, keeping his tone humorous. "Nobody's confused me about anything. How much longer till we reach the Bahamas again? This boat goes directly there, doesn't it?"

"Sure thing." Joshua smiled, clapping Tommy on the shoulder and winking at Lola. "We'll be sipping pina coladas as the new year comes in."

Tommy drove them off the ferry and headed for their cabin in the woods, which they'd taken over after Scott Frampton's brother, Chuck, had been convicted of theft and sent to prison a year and a half before. Since then, Lola and Tommy had made their cabin a cozy home, with a wood-burning fire, beautiful big-leafed plants that caught the sunlight just so, large paintings that Lola had collected from vintage shops, and plenty of toys and supplies for Max, Lola's ten-month-old grandson. Tommy had taken to Max like a funny uncle, sitting on all fours with him in the living room and playing with him or lifting him up to show him little twittering birds outside the window. Once, Audrey had referred to Tommy as "Grandpa Tommy," and Tommy had stiffened, looking shocked. Lola had asked Audrey privately not to call Tommy that again.

After the first snowfall, Tommy had shoveled a path through the glistening white from the driveway to the front door. Lola grabbed her suitcase and strolled up toward the door, where she collected the mail they'd missed over the previous few days from the mailbox and then headed inside. Once there, she put the kettle on the stovetop and checked her phone, which showed three missed calls: one from Audrey, one from Christine, and one from Susan.

Tommy entered and stomped off the snow from his boots before removing them and making his way into the kitchen in just his wool socks. He knelt to kiss Lola on the forehead before he grabbed himself a light beer from the fridge. Lola loved the ease they had with one another, now. She'd never had such beautiful synchronicity with a man. In fact, after all her chaotic relationships with men, she would have never imagined such a thing was possible.

Tommy sat at the kitchen table while Lola called her daughter back.

"Hi, Mom!" Audrey's voice was like a song. "Are you back on the Vineyard?"

"Just walked in the door," Lola told her. "Sorry I was MIA the past couple of days. It was a whirlwind."

"I'm sure it was." In the background, little Max squealed and then burst into laughter. "Sorry about that. Great-Grandpa Wes is trying to feed Max, and it's turning into comedy hour. Meanwhile, Susan and Christine are setting up everything for the party tonight. You're still coming, aren't you?"

"We wouldn't miss it," Lola assured her.

"Good." Audrey breathed a sigh of relief, then added, "Noah will probably stop by."

Lola lifted her eyebrows as a sharp wedge of curiosity pulled through her. "Is that so?"

"I hope it's not too big of a deal," Audrey said hurriedly. "The last thing I want is to distract everyone with my drama."

"There's no distracting," Lola returned. "We really like Noah. And you know what the Sheridan family wants more than anything, right?"

"More grandchildren?"

Lola laughed outright. How was it that Audrey could still surprise her with her quick wit? Shouldn't Lola have been used to it by then?

"No. We just want you to be happy," Lola replied.

Audrey had broken things off with her Vineyard-based boyfriend around Thanksgiving time when her life at Penn State had been crumbling around her. Now, with her life back on the Vineyard full-time, Audrey seemed to see no reason not to listen to her heart again.

Lola ended the call and then sat with Tommy for a little while, watching as a light snow filtered past the glossy windows outside. Both were wordless, and Tommy seemed lost in thought about his mother, the funeral events, and the work still yet to be done.

"You really don't have to come tonight," Lola finally told him. She could feel the deepening bruise of his heart.

"I want to be with you," Tommy told her softly, his eyes finding hers again.

"Even if being with me tonight means being with my loud and overwhelming family?"

"I love your loud and overwhelming family," Tommy told her, his smile widening. "You know that. It keeps my mind from wandering."

Around six, Tommy drove them back to the large cabin along the waterline, located next to the original Sheridan House. Scott had purchased the house and refurbished it prior to his and Susan's marriage. Now,

Scott, Susan, and Scott's teenage son, Kellan, lived there, with a host of others streaming in and out, depending on the needs of the greater Sheridan clan. During Christine's bedrest, for example, she'd taken up frequent residence; when their Aunt Willa had appeared out of the blue the previous month, she'd moved into Susan's guest bedroom and become another beautiful and nuanced member of the family, slowly coming into her own as her psychosis faded and memories of her husband's tragic death returned.

"We're expanding. Becoming a cult," Audrey had said after Scott had revealed his plans for the big house.

"At least we're well-fed," Christine had joked in return.

Much of the Sheridan and Montgomery family had already gathered at Susan's place to celebrate. The house edged toward "enormous," and the party operated on two floors before spilling out onto the enclosed porch, which offered a glorious view of the Vineyard Sound beyond. Lola and Tommy smiled joyously at the group of revelers — Lola's cousins, including the newlyweds, Andy and Beth and Beth's young son, Will, plus Kelli, Charlotte, Charlotte's boyfriend, the photojournalist, Everett, and her daughter, Rachel. Aunt Kerry stood in the corner with a large mug of hot mulled wine and greeted Lola and Tommy with a slurred, "Happy New Year to the beautiful couple!"

Susan sped through the crowd, her motions quick as a deer and her smile proof she was the perfect hostess. She wrapped Lola in a big-sister hug and then grabbed her and Tommy's coats. Tommy accepted a beer from Scott, who walked out of the kitchen with news of scores from a recent sporting event. Lola followed Susan into the next room to find Audrey, Max, Christine and her new baby, Mia, seated a bit away from the fireplace. Max lurked on all fours, licking his lips hungrily, his ocean-blue eyes catching the light of the fire as it flickered.

"He wants to stand and walk so bad," Audrey said, laughing as she stood to greet her mother with a hug.

"His little chunky legs won't let him," Christine returned. "Meanwhile, Mia is just content to watch all these strangers walking around her."

Indeed, the tiniest Sheridan lay in Christine's arms as her blue eyes darted left to right, watching as though she didn't dare trust anything about the world yet.

"She'll be down for a nap in another half hour," Christine told Lola as Lola perched alongside them, greeting Mia warmly. "She just wanted to stay up to say hi to Aunt Lola."

"Hello, little Mia," Lola whispered, taking Mia's little foot in hers. "Are you ready for a brand-new year?"

"She's only a week old," Christine said with a funny laugh. "She's hardly gotten used to this year yet." Christine's eyes then drew up toward the doorway, where Scott and Tommy were still in heavy sports talk. She lowered her voice to ask, "How is he doing?"

"He's okay. He has good and bad moments," Lola murmured. "I wasn't sure what to expect, but he's getting through."

"I'm surprised he came," Christine offered, her eyebrows creeping toward her forehead.

The hours inched toward the new year. Lola made herself a plate of cheesy potatoes, a favorite of hers since childhood. She then dove into the gossip and laughter, listening to Rachel's, Gail's, and Abby's tales from high school. Stories about Audrey's newfound journalistic success and the new updates on Kelli's rebuild of the Aquinnah Cliffside Overlook Hotel. Every half hour or so, Lola and Tommy checked in with one another, with Lola frequently saying, "If you want to get out of here, just say the word." Each time, Tommy shook his head.

Noah arrived to find Audrey at around ten. He lifted Audrey and whirled her around so that her feet extended out behind her, nearly reaching the Christmas tree in the corner. Susan's eyes nearly bugged out of her head at the sight, but she managed not to scream at Audrey. Crisis averted. Susan left the room in a flash to restock the cracker and cheese plate as Audrey continued to ogle Noah, her eyes filled with love and admiration.

Audrey wasn't the only one with a beau on New Year's Eve. Amanda, too, was privy to a surprise guest. Sam was hard at work at the Sunrise Cove Inn that night, and the two of them planned to have a celebration all their own on a night when Sam didn't have to manage the front desk. Still, during a slow moment at the Inn, Sam left Natalie at the front desk and whisked over to Susan's to give Amanda a pre-New Year's kiss. When Amanda returned to their little pow-wow near the fireplace, her cheeks burned red with a mix of embarrassment and passion. It had been nearly a year since her ex-fiancé had left her at the altar. Perhaps none of those sour memories remained.

"Everyone! It's nearly time!" Susan hollered excitedly at 11:57 p.m., demanding that the Sheridan and Montgomery families gather in the large living room with the fireplace to count down with the large grandfather clock and toast with champagne. The women of the house had poured enough champagne for everyone, plus sparkling grape juice for the kids and teenagers. They passed out the glasses as quickly as they could, as organized as flight attendants.

Tommy approached Lola with his champagne flute, his eyes not wavering and serious. Lola tried on a smile, but it fell from her face on impact. Around them, her family members spoke excitedly, teasing one another or gazing into one another's eyes, expectant for the big kiss at midnight. Lola wouldn't have been surprised if Tommy gave her only a peck on the cheek. After all, he wasn't necessarily the "showing his feelings" type of guy, and they had just returned from his mother's funeral.

"Ten. Nine. Eight..." The countdown began. Tommy's gritty voice beside Lola's gave her something powerful to hang onto. Tommy grabbed her hand and slipped his fingers through hers. Lola wanted to tease him, to ask him if he'd ever imagined he would want a New Year's Eve kiss, especially from the same woman two years in a row.

But just before the kiss, Tommy stepped in front of her, locked eyes with her, and then fell to one knee. Lola's heart dropped into her stomach. Around her, the Sheridan and Montgomery couples had come together, kissing and hugging and hollering out in celebration. All the while, Lola placed her hands on her cheeks in disbelief as Tommy's large, stoic eyes studied her. Through the chaos, he reached into his pocket and drew out a tiny black velvet box.

"Oh my God!" Audrey cried as she turned to find Tommy on one knee in front of her mother.

Slowly, everyone caught wind of what Tommy was about to do. They hushed up and watched as he popped open the velvet box to reveal an antique diamond ring, one that evoked beauty and timelessness all at once. Lola had never envisioned that anyone would ask her to marry him. She'd never had the fantasies, never imagined the ring or the scenario or what he might say.

"Lola Sheridan," Tommy said then. "Will you make me the happiest man on earth? Will you marry me?"

Chapter Three

That night, Lola's answer to Tommy's sudden question of marriage, a resounding YES, resulted in more popped champagne bottles, countless shrieks, impressive looks at the engagement ring, and several smacks on the back to Tommy, first from Scott, then from Zach, then from Grandpa Wes and Uncle Trevor and Cousin Andy. Lola remained latched to Tommy, her heart nearly bursting from her chest. Since her return to the Vineyard a year and a half before, she'd pushed the limits of her happiness. She wasn't sure if it could get much higher than this.

Audrey wept with surprise, throwing her arms around her mother as her body shivered. Lola sensed what her daughter thought. For nineteen years, it had been just the two of them against the world. The return to the Vineyard meant growing up for both of them— Audrey with her baby, Lola with her engagement, and both of them finding space for the enormous love they now had for their extended family. They could never return to that cozy ecosystem of the original Lola and Audrey show.

Soon after, Max's baby monitor gave out a resounding wail, and Audrey sped off to tend to him. There could be no waiting around and reminiscing. Life was happening all around them.

When Lola and Tommy returned to their cabin that night, they sat for a long time in the truck as though they wanted to extend the length of a night they would never forget. Lola gazed at him, wordless. Finally, she mustered the strength to say, "I thought you never wanted to."

To this, he returned, "Me neither. But with you by my side, I've become the kind of man I've always wanted to be. I've become stronger and more alive and more empathetic. It would be my honor to call you my wife. And I would be an idiot never to ask you. To be honest, I kind of thought you'd laugh in my face and tell me that Lola Sheridan isn't the marrying kind."

Lola's jaw dropped open with surprise. "You're making that up."

Tommy shrugged playfully before he leaned in for a kiss. "Maybe. Maybe I knew you'd say yes."

"Hey!" Lola whacked him on the shoulder, grinning as he kissed her. They both fell into heaps of laughter before they leaped out of the truck and headed into the cozy warmth of their cabin. "Would my fiancé like a glass of water?" she asked in the kitchen, poised at the counter.

Tommy's smile was electric. "Is my fiancée suggesting that I'm not hydrated enough?"

"I'm only saying that my fiancé is forty-six years old and not exactly keen on hangovers," Lola told him.

He took two large strides toward her and pressed her against the counter, using a bit more force than she'd expected. Her smile fell from her lips as she lifted her eyes toward his. This was to be the rest of her life.

The ring on Lola's finger was, in fact, a relic from a previous era and a previous continent. Apparently, it had belonged to Tommy's Italian grandmother, and his father had brought it over from Europe. "He never proposed to my mother with it." Tommy started to explain the history behind it. "But Mom told me that the ring was very important to him and that his grandparents' marriage was a powerful one, one that he wanted to emulate. Perhaps he did, somewhere across the Atlantic. But he left the ring here, perhaps as some sort of memento to his previous love for my mother and his sorrow for his inability to grow old with her."

Several days later, the end of the bed tipped low and lifted Lola from the calm of her sleep. She blinked through the darkness, sensing Tommy awake. Her hand wavered above the bedside table and turned the lamp on.

"I didn't mean to wake you," Tommy whispered, placing his hand over the covers above her ankle so that his fingers wrapped tenderly around the thin bone above her feet. "I got a text from Scott late last night, asking if I could work at the freight company this week."

"Ah." Lola blinked toward the harsh red light of the alarm clock, which read back 3:47 a.m. "You must be crazy."

Tommy chuckled. "You know I miss being out on the water more than anything. The freight's no sailboat, but it's at least something. And I'm useless while hanging around the Vineyard waiting for the winter to pass."

Lola pulled her legs out from under the blankets and hustled toward him, burrowing her head against the warmth of his chest. The thudding of his heart filled her skull. "Let me make you a pot of coffee," she whispered. "I'll hurry."

Lola leaped up and headed to the kitchen, where she brewed a large pot of black coffee while Tommy took one of his classic soul-crushing ice-cold showers. His cheeks were as bright as Christmas bulbs when he appeared at the kitchen table. He bent to draw his thick wool socks along his massive feet in an intimate performance. Still down there, he murmured, "I've given some thought to the wedding."

"Oh yeah?" The coffee pot bubbled and spat as the last of the black liquid oozed through the filter.

"I see no reason we should wait," Tommy told her, finally lifting his head. "All my life, I've thought of marriage as this prison. Who would ever want that? Now, I'm eager to lock the door and throw away the key as quickly as possible."

"You sound like some of my girlfriends at the end of college," Lola teased. "Thinking if they weren't married by twenty-three, they'd be labeled as old maids."

"I think that ship has sailed," Tommy told her.

"*Tra il dire e il fare c'e di mezzo il mare,*" Lola tried, her Italian accent soft and inarticulate yet nearly musical.

"Between doing and saying is half a sea. I know," Tommy said, his smile crooked. As he rose to kiss her, he breathed, "What about February?"

"You are eager," Lola returned with a laugh.

"Are you saying you need a little more time to think?" Tommy teased, bucking toward the door, forgetting the coffee altogether. "Are you saying you're not so sure about me?"

"Tommy!" Something about the wretched chilly dark-

24

ness outside led Lola back toward him. She flung her arms around him, yearning to threaten to make him stay in bed with her forever.

His smile was warm, soft behind his thick sailor's beard. "Say you'll marry me in February."

"I'll marry you tomorrow if Charlotte can plan it in time," Lola breathed before she dipped her head back for a final kiss.

Lola listened to the sound of Tommy's truck engine as she sat at the kitchen table with a large mug of coffee steaming before her. She positioned her feet on the edge of the chair and formed herself into a tight little ball. The bed beckoned her back into its warm folds, but her mind whirred gently, coming alive as the minutes passed.

With her laptop opened wide before her, Lola dug into the meat of a story she'd been working on for the Boston-based restaurant magazine. They had asked for a feature on the up-and-coming restaurants in Oak Bluffs and Edgartown. To her surprise, her language was articulate, her voice sharp as she sizzled through paragraphs three through eight. When she lifted her chin from the sterile glow of her laptop, she caught the first sunlight of morning as it beamed through the glorious forest.

Without giving it another thought, Lola grabbed her phone and texted her wedding planner cousin, Charlotte, who'd once planned the entirety of a celebrity wedding in three weeks flat (a feat that had projected her into wedding planning royalty).

> LOLA: Hey lady. How's your schedule in February? Am I crazy to ask you to plan a small (50-75 guests) wedding by then?

It was nearly seven, which meant Charlotte was guaranteed to be up with her teenage daughter, Rachel, scrambling through the frantic events of another early morning before school. She wrote back in three minutes, probably over-promising on a feat that seemed, to Lola, nearly impossible.

> CHARLOTTE: What a relief!
>
> CHARLOTTE: I was terrified you'd ask for a summer wedding. My summer's nearly all booked.
>
> CHARLOTTE: February, on the other hand? Not exactly wedding season on Martha's Vineyard.
>
> CHARLOTTE: Why don't we meet later this week to discuss your vision for the ceremony?
>
> CHARLOTTE: Gosh, you and Tommy are just about the hottest couple on this island. Everyone always told me he wasn't good news, you know. And I just told them they don't know Lola Sheridan like I do. You're just as bad news as Tommy. I suppose that's why it works.

Christine texted not long after to ask if Lola wanted to meet at the Sunrise Cove Bistro for a round of croissants and coffee. Lola leaped into the shower, fresh off three hundred precise and edited words and a nearly-set marriage date. She brushed through her luscious brown hair and tore through her fully stocked closet, something that, unfortunately, she'd felt to be slightly too youthful since the coming of Max Wesley Sheridan. She wasn't ageist; she was simply wary of coming off silly. It was something she'd have to discuss with her sisters at length. Not today, though. Today was a day for long flowing skirts, tight turtlenecks, and thick-soled boots. It was a day for overindulgences and gut-busting laughter. It was yet another day in the beautiful story of her love.

Audrey and Max awaited Christine and Lola in the Bistro dining area. Max sat in a high chair with a plastic spoon in hand. His big blue eyes found Lola and widened immediately with surprise and joy.

"Gosh, I wish I could bottle that feeling," Lola said as she greeted him with a kiss on the forehead. "He won't look at us like that forever."

Audrey stood and hugged her mother as Max threw the spoon onto the floor.

"I love the looks," Audrey admitted with a smile. "But the throwing game he's just come up with? I'm not a big fan of that, to be honest."

"Well, how else do you expect him to get that football scholarship?" Lola teased.

Audrey rolled her eyes and collected the plastic spoon. "Max Wesley is no football player. He's more of a beat poet. Isn't that obvious?"

"You can't plan out your child's future. They'll only surprise you and go the opposite direction," Lola said as she sat across from Audrey.

"Yeah?" Audrey's smile was mischievous. "Then what happened with me? I'm a journalist, just like you; we live ten minutes from each other, and I'm happier than I've ever been."

Lola's heart lifted into her throat. "You broke the mold."

After the server brought them two mugs of coffee and two glasses of orange juice, Christine entered the Bistro tentatively, with little Mia wrapped tightly against her chest. Despite her forty-three years and new-mother status, Christine looked fresh and vibrant, her skin glowing and youthful. Lola remembered all the mothers she'd spoken to over the years who'd called pregnancies after thirty-five "geriatric." What an alienating term. She was grateful Christine had paid it no mind.

"There they are. The most beautiful women in the room," Lola greeted Christine, rising up to hug her gently as Christine joined.

"She looks peaceful right now," Christine agreed. "But tell that to the version of her at one in the morning. Zach's still knocked out on his back, snoring on the couch. After his years in the restaurant industry, you'd think he'd be able to handle all kinds of complaints. His new daughter is his downfall."

The three adults and two babies settled in for a beautiful brunch as soft snow settled across the rolling hill that led toward the Vineyard Sound beyond. They ordered eggs Benedict, stacks of blueberry pancakes, and large, cloud-like croissants and spoke quietly over baby Mia's head. Even Max snoozed soon after his arrival and allowed himself to be placed gently in his baby carrier.

Audrey spoke about her new semester of online classes through Penn State, which had been specially set up for her after her newfound success as a journalist. She'd revealed the horrific secrecy of a particularly evil electric power plant, which had covered up decades of accidental deaths. One of the men who'd lost his life was their Aunt Willa's husband, a tragedy that had resulted in a loss of her memory and a retreat to Martha's Vineyard.

"The Penn State newspaper has agreed to give me a weekly column," Audrey explained as she smeared butter on a slice of her croissant with her knife. "I had this idea that I wanted to represent people like myself—

students off-campus who are still very much involved with Penn State. Every week, I plan to interview a different student about their majors, life goals, and particular situations. This week, I'm interviewing a twenty-five-year-old woman in Alaska who works at a little diner with a view of Mount Foraker and studies microbiology in her spare time. Her father has cancer, and she requested to do her course load online to stay home to be with him."

Christine's daughter lifted a tiny pink hand toward the sky as Audrey finished her story. Christine chuckled and nodded toward it, saying, "Mia approves of this woman."

"And of your brilliant idea for this column," Lola agreed. "How do you find students to interview?"

"Mostly Penn State message boards," Audrey explained. "People write to one another for advice on various projects or talk about the occasional 'loneliness' of living off-campus and away from everyone else. Although I hated last semester, it's felt strange not going back, yet still performing the same homework duties and watching classes online. It's like performing a play off-stage without a costume."

"We love having you here," Christine told her firmly.

"Especially now since I'll need your help with the wedding," Lola rushed out this news before she took a sip of coffee.

Audrey's eyes widened. "Are you suggesting that you have a date? I thought for sure you'd push that off as long as possible."

"You wouldn't hold out on us, would you?" Christine demanded.

Lola shrugged playfully. "It just might have been

suggested by one Tommy Gasbarro... that we marry in February. The sooner, the better."

Audrey's jaw dropped. "You're kidding."

"Miss 'I'm Never Getting Married' has decided to jump in headfirst!" Christine shook her head as her long locks cascaded across her shoulders. "Now, I'll be the only holdout."

"You skipped a few steps, I think," Lola returned, grinning toward little Mia, whose pink hand curled into a fist.

"We Sheridan women don't do anything in the correct order," Audrey stated, beaming down at Max in his carrier.

"It's because we're artists at heart," Christine agreed, half-teasing.

"Dancing to the beat of our own drum." Lola laughed.

"I wouldn't have it any other way," Audrey chirped.

Chapter Four

sharp January wind sliced across Lola's cheeks. She carried Max's carrier as Audrey leafed through her pocket for her car keys, listening for the jangle. Christine appeared behind them, her figure bulbous with the puffy winter coat, something she joked she would never have been caught dead in back in New York City. As they walked through the snow toward Audrey's car, Christine suggested she didn't feel quite like heading home yet.

"All I've done all week long is sit on that godforsaken couch," she explained. "And I swear, if Zach's still fast asleep on that thing, I might scream."

Audrey laughed appreciatively, as having a ten-and-a-half-month-old was no picnic, either. "I don't have to run home just yet. Aunt Kerry's at the house all morning with Grandpa Wes. Amanda said she'll be back home later this afternoon for another round of gossip, which I wouldn't miss for anything."

"What could we do?" Lola asked, tilting her head. "At

fifteen degrees, I'm not sure I'm terribly keen on going for a walk."

Christine and Audrey caught one another's eyes and shared a giddy, secretive grin. Lola's heart performed a backflip.

"What are you two up to?" she demanded.

"Get in, loser," Audrey instructed Lola, pressing her finger against her key fob to unlock the car door. "To quote the timeless classic, *Mean Girls*, 'We're going shopping.'"

Christine headed back to her car to collect the baby carrier and soon returned to latch it safely in the rear on the other side of Max. Both Max and Mia continued to sleep deeply. Occasionally, Max's eyes rushed back and forth behind his eyelids as though he hunted for something or someone in a dream world. Christine sat in the middle of both baby carriers while Lola buckled herself up front.

"I hate it," Christine moaned as she glanced down toward her stomach. "When I have Mia on my chest, I can pretend this lumpy belly isn't attached to me. But when I sit..."

"There it is," Audrey affirmed as she turned the key and roared the engine. "I remember that well."

"Your baby bump went away in two seconds flat," Christine said.

Audrey shivered. "I agree I was young, yes, but I'm also not sure your body ever fully goes back to normal after carrying a child for almost ten months and then giving birth."

Christine dropped her head back on the car seat as Audrey eased them through the slightly icy parking lot outside the Sunrise Cove. Already, Sam was out with a large bag of salt, helping one of the Sunrise Cove's maintenance workers to de-ice the parking lot. The temperature dropped quickly, dangerously transitioning from soft snow to something far more sinister.

Just as Lola's mind began to drift toward Tommy and her fears surrounding his life out on the water, she received a text message with a selfie of him, all bundled up on the top deck of the freight. Snow whipped around him, white and fluffy, and his eyes gleamed beautifully with proof of his joy.

> TOMMY: It's looking like I'll be working this job for the next couple of months.

> TOMMY: I can't say I can complain.

> TOMMY: Although it's true what Joshua said, that I've lost my head. Normally, I'm drinking a fruity alcoholic drink on some beach for all of January. Oh well.

> TOMMY: Love you, Lola. I'll see you later today.

"Look at this crazy man," Lola said as she flashed the photograph toward her daughter at a stoplight. "I guess I'll be married to him soon."

To Lola's immense surprise, Audrey drove them directly to the Edgartown wedding dress shop. It featured a wide selection of gorgeous and detailed vintage dresses, beautiful newly crafted dresses from fresh and local designers, and several bohemian looks that suited Lola's hungry eyes.

"You know that I've never tried on a wedding dress," Lola whispered, mystified at the experience as Audrey parked in the front row of the lot, which was more or less abandoned. "Let alone pictured myself in one."

"I know that," Audrey replied, her smile widening. "But it's looking like you're going to need one. And there's no time like the present, is there?"

Once inside, the woman at the front desk, dressed in a cream-colored power suit, introduced herself as Sara and greeted them warmly. She instructed them on where to place their baby carriers, where both Max and Mia remained in a deep sleep, and then discussed Lola's particular "vision" for her approaching "big day." The entire performance felt surreal. Lola shivered as she lifted her thumb and first finger to the glossy white fabric of a dress that had been hand-sewn in the year 1944. How many beautiful women on the precipice of the rest of their lives had worn this very dress?

One by one, Sara, Audrey, and Christine collected dresses for Lola. At the same time, Lola hung back, over-whelmed with the splendorous gowns and the possibility of looking like a fool in front of all of her and Tommy's families and friends. Tommy wasn't exactly a man of flourishes and frills. Perhaps he'd take one look at her and run the other way. She'd witnessed Amanda's fiancé dart from the altar and literally take on a new life halfway around the world. The story was enough to terrify any woman in the dark of night.

"Come on, Mom. Just try on one or two?" Audrey begged.

"Ugh, fine," Lola replied, her heart skipping a beat. She made her way into the dressing room and selected an A-line bohemian number in eggshell white with tiny buttons that went up the back. She removed her skirt and turtleneck and stepped delicately into the gown, dragging the little sleeves over her shoulders. As it wasn't yet fitted to her frame, it looked like she'd donned a fluffy cloud.

As she scrutinized her appearance in the mirror, the bell over the front door jangled as new guests entered. Lola froze, petrified. The last thing she wanted was for people outside of her family circle to see her looking like some kind of crazy wedding-obsessed princess.

"Hello!" the new guests greeted Sara. "We have an appointment?"

"Wonderful. You must be Penelope, Greta, and Margorie," Sara returned brightly.

"Penelope's the bride," a middle-aged woman explained.

"What's the date?" Sara asked.

"July ninth," Penelope replied, her voice a nervous whisper.

"Oh, good. We have some time, then," Sara said. "I've already set aside a few dresses based on your particular interests. Right this way."

Suddenly, the curtain between Lola and the big wide world erupted open. Audrey stood, vibrant and mischievous, her eyes swallowing the image of her mother whole. Lola's throat constricted with shame.

"Audrey!"

"Mom! You look amazing."

"Audrey, seriously?" Lola reached for the curtain to tug it back, but before she could, the three newcomers eyed her and beamed joyously.

The older women were both in their forties or early fifties, while Penelope looked to be mid-to-late twenties. After they introduced themselves, it was revealed that Greta, unfortunately, walked with crutches and had her left foot lifted, encased in a boot. Margorie appeared to be her sister, as the two were nearly identical.

"Look at you!" Greta cried warmly.

Lola's blush crept along her neck and cheeks. "I don't know. I feel a bit foolish."

"Why?" Penelope demanded. Probably, with her peach skin and her beautiful figure and her youth, she'd never felt this foolish in her life.

"She was never supposed to be the marrying kind," Christine explained. "She's coming to terms with it."

Greta crept forward on her crutches, smiling. "I didn't marry Penelope's father until I was thirty-five," she explained. "We always said marriage wasn't for us. Just a show thing. But Penelope told us how important it was to her that we become a real family."

Lola nodded warmly, grateful for the beauty of other people's very real and intimate stories. "My daughter's father took off, thank goodness. He left me with a baby and an unknown future ahead of me."

Greta laughed good-naturedly. "And now you're here. Must feel like a whirlwind."

"It does," Lola replied as she took an unconscious step out of the dressing room and then eyed herself in the large three-paneled mirror. The result wasn't perfection; in fact, it was far from a vision. Even still, there was a particular kind of magic in witnessing yourself in a wedding dress for the first time, even at forty years old. Lola's breath caught in her throat.

"Come on," Penelope all but ordered her. "Let's try on more together. We can give each other moral support."

Bit by bit, Lola's feelings of silliness ebbed away, leaving only laughter, funny conversation with the rest of the women in the wedding dress shop, and a beautiful expectation for the weeks ahead. Not a single dress was perfect, not that snow-filled morning. But perhaps soon, her eyes would dance across the perfect shade and the ideal style. Perhaps soon, she'd be the ideal bride.

"Gosh, I need to readjust," Greta said as she shifted on the cushioned chair in the dressing room area. "This boot is a nightmare. I haven't gotten used to it yet."

Christine began to undo Lola's back buttons as Lola asked, "Is this a new injury?"

"Yes, only a week ago," Greta affirmed, the color fading from her cheeks. "I slipped on the ice. You'd have thought me, a born and bred Vineyard girl, would have known better, but nope!"

"It was terrifying," Margorie informed them. "I was right there when it happened and honestly felt so helpless."

"Gosh, I'm sorry," Lola returned.

"It's really messed up a lot this year," Greta continued. "Especially because I was supposed to direct the community theater production of *Annie*. Auditions were slated to begin in just a few days, but instead, I had to email everyone that we're calling it off."

"You couldn't find anyone else to direct?" Christine asked.

Greta shook her head. "It's so much work and takes a lot of time, so if you have a full-time job, it's not likely you can take it on. Besides, the people already invested in community theater want to be on stage performing and not behind the scenes. It's the only ego boost for Martha's Vineyard thespians we have."

"I didn't even know there was a community theater scene on the Vineyard," Audrey piped up, looking around at the ladies.

"Oh yes," Greta replied, her eyes glowing. "Last year, we put on *Jesus Christ Superstar,* and goodness, it was a thrill. I still wake up singing some of those songs. The cast was particularly talented that year. Devastatingly, one of our most passionate actors in the community theater passed away just a few days after our final performance. Nobody knew it would be his last musical— it tears me up inside to think about his dear wife, Cora. The two of them performed in twenty-five different community theater productions over the years, often as the two main leads."

Lola's heart squeezed with dread. A strange voice in the back of her head reminded her of the permanence of marriage— that ultimately, "till death do us part" had a terrifying ending. What did it mean to be left alone in life when your love abandoned you for whatever came next?

"Mom, remember when we did all those community theater productions back in Boston?" Audrey started, twirling on her front toe.

"What?" Christine gasped. "I didn't know that."

"Oh yes. Mom killed it," Audrey continued. "Remember when you played Eliza in *My Fair Lady?* You practiced that accent for ages. You must remember it."

Lola's brain cut through the memories as her tongue lifted to perform a cockney accent. *"All I want is 'enry 'iggins's 'ead."*

Greta's jaw dropped as laughter flourished through the wedding dress shop.

"You didn't forget!" Audrey cried. "All you did was say nonsense words for months."

"What did you even say?" Christine demanded.

"All I want is Henry Higgins's head," Lola replied with a shrug. "It was hard to get the H back after the performance since I had to drop it for the role."

"I was always some little girl or another in these productions," Audrey explained. "Always sitting with a coloring book, watching Mom absolutely tear through whatever song and dance number she had next. I kind of forget why we stopped doing them?"

Lola shrugged. "My career picked up in my late twenties. I couldn't squeeze in rehearsals anymore."

Greta nodded as her eyes widened. "Do you miss it?"

"To be honest, I haven't thought about it very much," Lola told her. "Not until now."

With her buttons undone, Lola returned to the dressing room to grab her street clothes and transition back into her real self. Outside the dressing room, Greta and Margorie whispered mysteriously, and Penelope spoke to Sara about the importance of finding the correct drop waist for the length of her torso. When Lola returned the last wedding dress to the rack, she curiously found Greta peering at her.

Lola tilted her head. "That look is dangerous, isn't it?"

Greta chuckled. "Not unless you want it to be. My sister and I were talking about you. About your background in theater."

"Uh-oh," Lola said.

"How's your workload these days?" Greta asked.

Lola's eyes shifted toward Audrey, who leaped up and down with excitement. "You got me into this," Lola told Audrey pointedly. "You know better than to bring up my theatrical past!"

"Mom..." Audrey howled. "What if you love it? Isn't this the year of trying new things? Pushing boundaries?"

"I'm already getting married, Audrey," Lola pointed out. "Isn't that enough?"

"Why not do everything at once?" Greta added, her grin widening. "Plus, I'd love nothing more than to email the community theater troupe and let them know that I found a stand-in director."

Lola groaned to herself while shaking her head. "What's the schedule like?"

"The performances are set for February twenty-fourth, twenty-fifth, and twenty-sixth," Greta explained. "We've had the auditorium space booked for a year. It would be a shame to waste it."

"And didn't you say you and Tommy want your wedding around that time, as well?" Christine asked.

Lola's smile curled toward her ears. Hope and expectation beamed out from Greta's and Margorie's eyes. With Tommy off on his freight liner over the next few months and Lola's journalism stories no more than ten hours per week, Lola felt herself actually considering this huge time suck as a viable option.

"Please, Mom! I'll help you when I have time," Audrey pleaded, clasping her fingers together. "I'll even rope Amanda in."

"I'm sure she'll be pleased that you've added her to the equation without asking her," Lola teased.

"All Amanda ever does is sing when no one's around," Audrey replied. "She's obsessed with musical theater. Frankly, it's annoying. I need to give her an outlet."

"And again, I can't even translate to you how pleased the people of the community theater troupe would be..." Greta said softly.

"Giving back to your community? The beauty of musical theater? The power of directing for the first time?" Audrey recited these points, ticking them off across her fingers. "I don't see any downsides, Mom."

Lola groaned inwardly and dropped her head back. "Oh gosh. Fine. Fine. I'll do it." She then made eye contact with Audrey, who beamed from ear to ear. "But you and your pal Amanda had better pull your weight. This is a family affair now."

Audrey saluted her, standing pin-straight like a soldier. "We live to serve you, Director Sheridan. Whatever you say goes."

Chapter Five

The chime on Cora Randall's cell phone was not, as she'd assumed, an indication that it was time to take the single-serving lasagna dinner from the oven. When she opened the oven, she found a half-frozen slab of vegetarian lasagna, something Victor would have referred to as "rabbit food." Knowing he'd been taken from this world due to a bad heart was a curse. If only she'd forced a little more rabbit food here and there. If only she'd swapped roast beef for Brussels sprouts. If only.

She soon learned that the chime just then was an alert for an email. This was a surprise. Cora hardly received emails these days, especially as she'd decided to retire from her career at the high school after her husband's death. Everyone had told her to hang onto her job— that it would keep her going day after day. But to Cora, it had seemed meaningless, performing the rituals of an ordinary life while her insides bungled themselves up with the weight of her depression. Besides, who wanted to spend more time with high schoolers than they had to?

The email was from Greta Collins, the director of community theater productions for the previous twelve years. Over a week ago, it had been announced that Greta had been injured, destroyed her foot, and couldn't perform her duties as a director any longer. This, to Cora, seemed in line with the rest of her world, as everything had shifted off its axis. Why should she have musical theater back? It wouldn't have felt right without Victor by her side on stage, anyway.

Cora opened the email prepared for an update on Greta's health. But what she found instead was rather surprising.

Dear Thespians of Martha's Vineyard,

It pleases me to write this email. I've just had a bout of good luck. Call it serendipity. Call it fate. Call it whatever you want! But I've found the stand-in community director for this year's production of Annie— *and she's perfect for the gig.*

Lola Sheridan is the youngest daughter of Wes and Anna Sheridan (of the Sunrise Cove Inn). At thirty-eight, she returned to our beautiful island after twenty years away. She's a renowned journalist, a killer dresser, and a seasoned thespian herself.

Therefore, auditions will go on as originally planned throughout the afternoon and evening of Friday, January 7th, beginning at 4 p.m. sharp.

Again, it is a real tragedy for me to miss out on this truly spectacular role as your director. Know that I will be there in the audience rooting for you throughout the final weekend of February, and that, God willing, I will be back in the director's chair come autumn, when we're slated to put on Who's Afraid of Virginia Woolf?

All my love to you, my thespians. And break a leg at auditions! Not a foot, like I did.

Greta

Cora read the email twice more, positioned her phone on the countertop, and headed for the study. Once seated at the computer Victor had purchased for them seven years previous, she sought out the Sunrise Cove Inn's website to read about the family history of the old place. When Cora was in her late twenties, she'd heard the wretched story of Anna Sheridan's death— a boat accident off the coast of Edgartown. She'd left three girls behind. On the website, Cora now read about those three adult women who helped out at the Sunrise Cove Inn alongside their chosen careers. The description featured a photograph of the three women alongside their father, Wes Sheridan, who was now in his seventies. He was still handsome, proud, with his chin lifted high as his cerulean eyes caught the sunlight that beamed over them as if blessing them.

All those years ago, he'd lost his wife in a tragedy—the love of his life.

Unlike Cora, however, he had proof of their love with his gorgeous daughters and, it seemed, a number of grandchildren.

There was no way Cora would audition for this silly musical, right? Her daily schedule suited her just fine. She saw the occasional friend, did the crossword every afternoon, always had a book going, and had a number of TV shows scattered throughout the week. This, she'd found after Victor's death, was a surprising way to keep her expectations up. As long as she made it to Thursday, she could piece together the missing links left over from the crime show the week before. As long as she made it to

Saturday, she could watch the black-and-white movie marathon, which highlighted films she hadn't seen since she'd been a little girl. At fifty-seven, it felt remarkable to face old age with such a textured life behind her. So many people had passed away. So much had come and gone.

"You're a star, kid." This was what Victor had said after each performance— no matter the audience. He'd said it after their performances at the Oak Bluffs auditorium. He'd said it after she sang her solo in the church choir. He'd said it after she'd retreated from singing in the shower.

"Your gift is your voice. And you should be sharing it with the world." Her mother had told her this when she'd been a little girl, auditioning for the elementary school play.

Cora received a phone call from her neighbor, a woman named Henrietta. Henrietta often checked in on Cora as though Cora was an invalid who needed word from the outside. Cora had grown to resent these phone calls, but if she resisted them, Henrietta usually took it upon herself to just come over instead— usually with a bottle of wine and some banana bread. Cora found it difficult to get her out of her house once she came in. She was like bed bugs.

"Hi there, Cora. I was just thinking about you. I made all these lemon bars and thought to myself, who might want these? And I thought of you."

Cora's throat tightened. She had to avoid human contact with this woman at all costs. She stuttered and said, "Oh, I don't know about that. Don't you want to give them to your grandchildren?"

"Nonsense. They get enough sugar as it is. I've told you how I feel about their mother. She feeds them nothing but those packaged meals— the overprocessed nonsense."

"Mm-hmm." Cora's eyes widened.

"I heard a rumor that the theater production won't go ahead this year," Henrietta continued. "It broke my heart to know that we wouldn't be able to see your lovely presence on stage, but then I said to myself, isn't that a blessing in a way? How I love to sit at your house and while away the time with you. Retirement isn't so bad when you have people to share it with."

Cora found it terribly difficult to breathe. She closed her eyes and reached for Victor's old pipe, which she'd had cleaned and positioned just to the left of the computer. It was beautifully carved mahogany wood; her finger could sense the countless times he'd lifted the pipe to his lips, drawing it and then puffing out smoke. It was heavy with the past.

She could half believe he was on his way to retrieve it from the study, to tease her about how she'd insisted he stop smoking the thing in the house.

Just let him walk down the hallway to tease her.

Just let him come in and say anything at all.

"Stop chatting with Henrietta if you don't want to. Nobody put a gun to your head."

"Your life is your own, Cora. Nobody's going to live it for you."

"Is this how you want to spend your life, Cora? Waiting around for me to come back? That's not the woman I married."

"Actually," Cora heard herself blurt out, "they've just found a stand-in for the director. The youngest Sheridan girl will be covering for Greta."

"Oh! Lola Sheridan. Is that so? You know, she lives

with that man who is always sailing his boat, and I don't think they're married," Henrietta continued. "Such a strange sinful life, the sailor's life. I can't imagine that Lola girl was up to much good when she left the island, either."

"I can't speak to her actions, Henrietta," Cora returned dryly. "All I know is that I have to prepare the best piece for my audition if she's going to cast me as anything at all."

Cora leaped off the phone call just as the oven beeped, alerting her to take out the vegetarian lasagna. Although the ice had melted off and the noodles had softened, it still looked like slops in a pig trough. Before Victor's death, Cora had constructed elaborate and beautiful meals, soufflés, homemade pasta, and even self-rolled sushi. What had happened to her? Would she really cease all signs of life?

Would she really live for the Thursday evening crime shows, the black-and-white movie marathons, and the afternoon crosswords? Was that what Cora Randall was all about?

Cora returned to the study to print out sheet music from the musical *Annie*. At the age of fifty-seven, Cora knew herself to be perfect for one incredibly important and juicy role within the musical itself. Miss Hannigan was the greedy and monstrous leader of the orphanage. She was a woman whose mega eye rolls could be witnessed from the farthest seat away in the auditorium. Her gut-busting solos were the stuff of legends. And what was more, it sounded silly and quite fun to work alongside little "orphan girls" at the orphanage, especially because, well—

If Cora was honest with herself, she'd always really wanted children, hadn't she?

It just hadn't happened for her.

Well, not in a traditional way, at least.

Cora positioned the sheet music for "Tomorrow" atop her piano and splayed her hands tenderly across the keys. Her mother had gifted her weekly lessons throughout her youth, but her passion for the keys had faltered as she'd launched into singing, theater, and dance. For one tear-filled year, she'd studied theater at Boston University, but she had missed the Vineyard (and Victor) so desperately that she'd returned. When Victor had asked if she regretted her departure from school, Cora had nearly laughed. "I never think about it," she'd told him. "I only think about the life we've built here together. And the fact that we're able to share the stage together side by side, year after year. Maybe if I'd been an actress in New York City, I would have had one or two okay-ish roles before giving up for good. And who knows. By then, you might have found a far better wife to call your own."

At this, Victor had scoffed. "As if. Now, you're talking nonsense."

Cora spent the next few days practicing for her audition. She felt like a well-oiled machine with a real purpose to get up in the morning.

On Friday, January seventh, Cora arrived at the audition fifteen minutes before four and sat in the parking lot doing breathing exercises until the auditorium door was unlocked. As she inhaled, exhaled, inhaled, exhaled, she watched as several previous cast members stepped out of their vehicles and headed for the door. They looked nervous with excitement. There was Harold, a man in his fifties who'd frequently drank Manhattans with Cora and

Victor back at their place after rehearsal. There was Francesca, a woman in her late thirties who'd taken on several important roles over the past years of community theater, including once playing Victor and Cora's daughter in a production. This had been a remarkable time for Cora and Victor, as they'd taken the opportunity to grow closer to Francesca and treat her like an "adopted daughter." Francesca had been overjoyed with their friendship, but she'd slowly drifted away over the years, especially as she started a family of her own.

Cora gathered her materials and walked down the long sidewalk that led into the auditorium. Once inside, memories assaulted her in all directions— scenes that she hadn't considered in many years, scents that made her head ring with Victor's voice, along with sights that reminded her of countless other roles and memorized lines. She staggered forward before straightening herself, not wanting to be seen as the crazy woman she knew she could become if she wasn't careful. Lonely widows were apt to fall through the cracks.

A young woman with Sheridan features greeted her warmly and handed her a pamphlet, on which was listed the order of people auditioning. The young woman began to describe the process, but Cora nodded almost immediately and said, "This isn't my first rodeo." The young woman laughed graciously and extended her arm toward the auditorium. "Then take a seat. We'll get started very soon."

At three minutes past four, Lola Sheridan, along with the young woman who'd handed out the pamphlets and another young woman with similar features (all this dark hair, ocean-blue eyes, slender figures— the family seemed taken from a catalog), stepped up on stage to greet everyone who was ready to audition. Lola Sheridan seemed nervous, swapping her weight from leg to leg.

"Thank you for coming here today," Lola greeted them. "I trust that many of you have auditioned before. For the rest of you, the process goes like this. You'll hand off your music to Rhonda, our gracious and talented pianist, and then tell us what you're auditioning for, then perform a little tune. If we like what we see today, we'll call you to read lines over the weekend. We hope to announce all parts by Sunday so we can dig into this beautiful, fun, and upbeat musical by this Monday afternoon."

Cora was listed as twelfth in line to audition. This gave her plenty of time to have a full-on freak-out as others jumped on stage to perform. Her old friend Harold sped up midway through his performance so that the pianist was left chasing after him as he barreled toward the end. Francesca sang quite sweetly, tenderly, but her eyes were glassy with fear. Three high schoolers walked on stage, one after another, and introduced themselves as Gail, Abby, and Rachel. All had no idea who they wanted to play in the musical. "Just one of the orphans, I guess," the last one said.

Two little girls auditioned for Annie prior to Cora's audition. One of them was eight years old with curly black hair and a big gap in her front teeth. She tap-danced across the stage joyfully, nearly flying through the air, flailing her arms. Her voice was less-than-stellar and wavered nervously between her lines. When she got off the stage, her mother scolded her, grabbed her hand, and dragged her back into the hallway. Cora rolled her eyes with disdain. Some parents didn't know what a beautiful life they'd been given. They couldn't comprehend the weight of their actions and words on the blossoming child before them.

Up on stage, Cora delivered the sheet music to Rhonda with a wink. Rhonda's jaw dropped with surprise. She hissed, "Someone told me you weren't coming back this year!"

Cora's smile was electric. There was something about stepping out on stage, especially after nearly a year away. Her body was light and airy, her smile eager and easy, and her posture pin-straight yet not militant. She felt glorious and feminine and ready to take on anything. She could have performed a one-woman show at that moment, given the time.

"Good afternoon, Cora," Lola Sheridan began from the dark seats below. "What will you be auditioning for today?"

Cora's voice was unrecognizable, at least to herself. It was musical and easy.

"I'll be auditioning today for the part of Miss Hannigan," Cora replied gently, realizing that she wanted to create a contrast between her own personality and that of the character.

"All right. We're ready for you," Lola replied with a firm nod.

With that, Rhonda burst into "Little Girls," a Miss Hannigan lament that illustrated her raucous anger toward the little girls at the orphanage along with her alcoholism and her general greediness.

"Little girls. Little girls. Everywhere I turn, I can see them..." Cora began, scrunching her face, building angst. Her voice became guttural and feminine as she grew louder, strutting across the stage. *"I'd have cracked years ago if it weren't for my sense of humor..."*

Cora's performance drew her out of herself. It tore back the years and allowed her to feel thirty, thirty-five— during the years when she and Victor had been the king and queen of that very stage. And when, three and a half minutes later, she found herself at the edge of the song, her throat aching and her eyes alight, she gasped with immense pleasure and nearly crumpled into tears.

"Bravo!" Lola and the rest of the crowd waiting for their auditions howled. "Bravo!"

Cora gave a gentle bow and hustled out of the auditorium, suddenly sizzling with fear. Once outside in the frigid air, she placed her hand on the stone wall of the auditorium and lifted her chin toward the impenetrable blue sky. She'd forgotten her coat and her sheet music, but none of it mattered— not at this moment. For now, after nearly a year of no music at all, she finally felt alive.

Chapter Six

Auditions finished for the night by seven. After witnessing such tremendously talented (and not so talented, but still very brave) Martha's Vineyard residents on stage, belting out musical numbers like there was no tomorrow, Lola felt energized and inspired. As she and her assistant directors, Amanda and Audrey, headed out into the chilly darkness, they swapped tales of their favorite appearances from the previous three hours, gushing about the cute little tap dancer, the little ballerina girl who'd cried halfway through, and most importantly, the fifty-seven-year-old woman named Cora, who'd absolutely blown everyone else out of the water.

"That's who Greta was talking about at the wedding dress shop," Audrey said as she buckled herself into the back of Lola's car. "The one whose husband was also just as talented."

"Oh, that's right," Lola returned. She turned the engine on along with the heat and sat waiting as the fog lifted from her vehicle windows. "I nearly wept and cried at the same time during her performance. She and her husband must have really been something to see up there together."

Amanda groaned inwardly. "Casting Annie is going to be difficult."

"The most important part," Audrey affirmed from the back seat. "But you know what I think. That little girl whose mom freaked out after she messed up her solo wasn't that bad. Just nervous, I think."

"Difficult to ask children to take on such big roles," Lola muttered. "Audrey, you were always so terrified before each performance. I had to distract you backstage, singing little songs and twirling you around in circles."

"I remember that," Audrey noted softly, lost in a world of memory.

"If I'm being honest, it helped me, too," Lola breathed as she glanced in Amanda's direction. "My little girl and I, as we played pretend on stage in front of hundreds of people. It was a dream come true."

It was Friday night, the first of the year, and Susan Sheridan Frampton had convinced the entirety of the Sheridan clan to sit around her dining room table and celebrate the end of the week "as a family." This was where the three of them headed now.

"Mom's making chili," Amanda informed them after investigating her phone, where she'd received photos of the prep party from Susan. "And what looks to be enough cornbread to feed a small country."

"Good. I'm starving," Audrey hollered from the back. "All that auditioning took it out of me."

* * *

As they breezed through the back entrance of Susan's home, the smells of simmering spices and hearty bread enveloped them. A radio was playing old '80s tunes on the kitchen counter, and Christine was stationed near the pot with a big wooden spoon in hand. As Mia slept upstairs in the guest bedroom, her baby monitor was stationed nearby.

"Hello, darlings!" Christine called brightly. She then pointed her wooden spoon at the baby on the floor, who army crawled on all fours toward Audrey with more strength than a soldier. "He's getting so fast. It's hard to keep up with him!"

Audrey laughed as she bent down to collect the little boy and bob him against her. Christine informed her that he'd been fed and had eaten well. Audrey thanked her and then hustled upstairs to put him to sleep as well. Lola watched, her heart swelling with love as her daughter ran off to perform this thankless and timeless duty— a mother wishing her baby good night.

"There she is! The newest theater director of Oak Bluffs auditorium." Lola's father appeared at the back door with Kellan hot on his heels. He wore his puffy winter coat and his thick ear muffs. He paused to stomp out the snow from his boots before removing and positioning them to the side of the mud room.

"What were you two troublemakers out doing?" Lola asked as she lifted her lips to kiss her father's cheek.

"Kellan and I were out enjoying the last light," Wes replied. "And then we lost track of time as we wandered around the Sunrise Cove, talking about everything and anything." Wes then clapped the teenage boy on the shoulder, grinning like a teenager himself. "And we saw ourselves a real treasure, didn't we?"

Kellan nodded as he yanked his gloves from his chilly-looking fingers. "It's that same cardinal, I think. Grandpa Wes has seen him once a week since Thanksgiving."

"Darn right, I have," Grandpa Wes said with a snap of his fingers. "That cardinal and I have a real understanding. Very simpatico, that cardinal and I."

Lola chuckled. Her father's vitality oozed over when he spoke about the majestic nature of the birds of Martha's Vineyard. He spent hours strolling through the woods, his binoculars pressed against his eyes. Kellan had taken on the pastime as well, listening intently to his step grandfather's words and taking everything to heart.

"I hope I'll get to see him sometime," Lola said.

"Come with me to the woods," Wes returned excitedly. "The invitation is open any time, honey."

Susan hustled down the staircase, her hair frizzy and wild behind her. When she spotted Christine at the chili pot, she sighed deeply. "Goodness. I fell asleep and thought for sure that..."

"That nobody would check on the chili if it wasn't for you?" Christine teased. "You know, the rest of us know a thing or two about the kitchen."

"Christine might even work as a professional pastry chef," Lola added, her smile widening.

Susan, the older sister who needed to have the last word, tried to untangle her hair with her fingers as she heaved an additional sigh. "I've been so weighed down with this new case at the firm."

"Surprise, surprise," Lola shot as she headed for the kitchen sink to wash her hands. "Our Susan's a worker bee— saving the world, one criminal at a time."

Susan evoked her teenage self with a heavy eye roll, then walked past Lola to grab a big bag of barbecue chips and select two circular salty morsels, which she placed delicately on her tongue.

"Hey! Give me one of those," Christine cried.

"Me too!" Lola said.

"You'll spoil your appetite," Susan replied mischievously, just before Lola grabbed the bag of chips from her hands.

Wes entered the kitchen and poured himself a glass of water. Amanda joined to greet her mother and assist in a re-style of her messy hair.

"I'm sorry I had to leave early today. I didn't know you were in the middle of a meltdown," Amanda said to Susan. They worked together at the downtown Oak Bluffs law office of Sheridan and Sheridan. Amanda was still in law school but helped out on a number of cases and had built up a whip-smart résumé while at the firm.

"Not to worry! I want to hear all about the auditions when we sit down for dinner. As soon as we find everyone else, that is." Susan blanked and then headed out to the front porch, where she found Scott in the middle of a book he dreaded to tear himself away from.

"You know when you just get so involved in a story?" Scott began romantically as he joined the others, his eyes still lost in the dream.

"That's terribly sweet, honey," Susan returned quickly. "But I need you to get a big bag of ice for us from the garage."

Scott bent to kiss his new wife on the cheek before he sped back out to the garage to help out.

"Scott said Tommy's been a godsend at the freight company," Susan said as she began to remove big chili bowls to set the table.

"I haven't loved waking up around four in the

morning every day," Lola admitted. "But Tommy's happy to be out on the water again."

"Where is he tonight?" Susan asked. "Didn't he get the word about the family dinner?"

Lola grabbed some bowls from Susan's outstretched hands and headed toward the beautiful dining room table, which hadn't yet been set for enough people.

"He got word, all right," Lola said playfully. "But he's back in Boston tonight to start going through some of his mother's things."

"He's always all over the place, our Tommy," Susan remarked. "Although not as much as he used to be. I'll give him that."

Susan and Lola worked like a near-perfect synchronized diving team as they positioned the large blue bowls on either side of the table. They then scrambled back to the kitchen to fetch wineglasses and water glasses. There, they found a newly-returned Audrey and Amanda in the midst of describing the beautiful performance of Cora Randall, who'd nearly brought them both to tears.

"And this song that she sings, it isn't actually supposed to be that emotional," Amanda continued.

"Yeah. It's more fun. But her comedic timing was almost tragic. You could really feel that this woman was wasting her life at this orphanage. She had no other way to get by," Audrey explained while holding a hand to her chest for theatrics.

Grandpa Wes had very little concept of what took place in a musical theater production. Even still, he feigned interest and asked additional questions about Cora and the rest of the cast. Then he finished up with, "And what part will you give me? I'm clearly the star!"

Audrey and Amanda cackled joyously just as Aunt

Willa entered the kitchen, her smile bright and sleepy. The doctor had recently switched up her medicine which had brought greater clarity to her mind but had completely drained her energy levels. Even still, she was a marvelous person to be around, ever quick with a joke and a smile. She'd also really taken to both Max and Mia and never hesitated to offer to babysit. Like so many other women in the world, she had ached to be a mother, but it had never worked out for her.

Together, the Sheridan family sat around the dining room table, heaped their large bowls with chili, drank from bottles of red wine, and swapped even more stories from the first week of the year.

Amanda had taken on an elaborate case of her own at the Sheridan law offices, one that had required hours of research in estate law. Audrey had finished her interview with the Alaskan and Penn State student and now pieced the story together bit by bit as she scraped through the rest of her course load and prepared for the upcoming musical schedule. Aunt Willa was in the market to have an apartment of her own and had viewed three in a quaint little apartment complex in Edgartown only that afternoon. Grandpa Wes was reportedly "in love" with the woman who'd assisted him at his recent doctor's appointment, a story that made Susan, the one who'd been there for the appointment, roll her eyes. And Scott told a funny story about his long hours out on the water with Tommy, who had "more tales from around the world" than any other person he'd met in his life.

Lola fell into the warm haze of the evening, the textured bite of the chili, the laughter of her nearest and dearest. Her heart was expectant, light for the coming weeks— for the days of rehearsals, the nights of performance, and then finally, the ultimate night of her life, her marriage to Tommy.

When they'd decided to just throw the performances, the wedding, and Max's first birthday all in one weekend, Lola and Audrey had hollered with laughter.

"You always have to make everything just the slightest bit dramatic, don't you?" Audrey had teased.

"I don't see any other way to live."

"I feel just the same way. I suppose that's why you're my mother."

Chapter Seven

In the old days, cast lists were hung outside the auditorium at a specific time, usually five p.m. on the evening prior to the first rehearsal. About five years ago, this routine shifted. The cast list was now upgraded to an online version— which, in Cora's mind, took out a lot of the fun. She had fond memories of jumping into the truck with Victor and driving in silence all the way to the auditorium, both fearful and alive to see the results, their stomachs bubbling with expectation. Of course, nobody could have touched their talent with a ten-foot pole back then. That said, they still celebrated the parts they'd gotten as though they'd won the lottery, usually grabbing a bottle of champagne and dancing all through the night.

That was how it had been back then.

Now, at three in the afternoon on the day before the first rehearsal, Cora walked into the study wearing her slippers. She sat on the edge of the desk chair and clicked on the email link, which led her to the cast list.

Even still, despite the lack of pomp and circumstance,

she yelped with joy when Cora spotted her name —
CORA RANDALL — on the cast list as Miss Hannigan.
Her arms flung through the air as though they had minds
of their own, and before she knew it, she'd rushed down
the hall to find her cell phone, as certainly, she must have
someone to call.

But when she lifted the phone, her heart brimming
with this news, she could think of absolutely no one on
earth she wanted to tell this victory to.

Disheartened yet unwilling to give up, Cora headed
to the bathroom, showered, scrubbed herself up, donned
makeup and did her hair. Within the hour, she was
wearing Victor's favorite bright red dress and a pair of
high heels. She twirled before the floor-length mirror to
flourish her skirt around her in a wide, Marilyn Monroe-
inspired circle. She then grabbed the only bottle of champagne she had, donned her winter coat and hat and drove
out to the graveyard.

Cora had never been particularly fond of the real
world. Back in the old days, Victor had called her a
dreamer, one apt to reflect on the past and the future as
she drove all the way home, forgetting to run all the neces-
sary errands for the day. "Darn it. I forgot to grab milk,"
she would say dreamily as she floated through their house,
still lost in thought. She supposed this half-hearted feeling
she had about the "present" was why she acted so well in
the theater. Reality was just as far away from her as
fiction. She supposed, also, it was why she felt so at home
amongst the dead at the graveyard. But beyond all that,
the graveyard was where the love of her life was buried.
Why should she feel strange?

Victor was buried ten rows away from the parking lot
and thirty stones west of the shed where she frequently

spotted graveyard workers hovering together, their shovels positioned against the wooden wall and cigarettes between their fingers. Sometimes, she gave them a wave, and they returned with a nod. Probably, they referred to her as something by then— the Randall widow, perhaps, or the crazy loony lady who sat on the ground at her husband's grave and chatted with him about whatever was on her mind.

Still, due to their sheer proximity to it, their familiarity with loss lent them more empathy than your average Joe. Cora paid them no attention as she dropped to her knees at Victor's gravestone and outlined his name with her fingers, her heart pulsing quickly as she curved her nail along the sharp edge of the V and then circled the O twice. She and Victor had never discussed the specifics about things like gravestones or burial plots. At the time of his death, she'd been fifty-six years old, and he'd been only fifty-nine. They'd thought of themselves as youthful and lucky, their love and passion for one another as bright as the day they'd met. "We'll have entire days in bed during retirement," Victor had said numerous times. "Just like our twenties."

"Hi, Vic," Cora whispered, her voice rasping. "I came to celebrate with you, just like the old days." She then removed the bottle of champagne and carefully uncorked it. Only a smattering of bubbles coursed across her hand. She'd brought a single red plastic cup, like the ones they drank from in college movies, and filled it nearly to the brim. She then tipped the edge of the cup against the gravestone as she closed her eyes. In the darkness, she could make out the specifics of his handsome face and sense the subtle shift of emotion as he took on joy, sadness, or fear.

"You did it, Cora. You got the best gosh-darn part in the whole musical. And you're going to wow them every step of the way."

The edges of Cora's heart seemed permanently shattered. She lifted the champagne and took on the sharp flavor as her eyes pooled with tears. It seemed silly to remind him how much she missed him. It almost seemed like nagging. Ultimately, it was unfair to blame him for his untimely demise. Fate had little at all to do with what Victor Randall had wanted.

Cora turned to the smaller, more weathered stone just to the right of Victor's grave and placed a hand delicately on this other name. Over the years, this name had become like a song for her— a song sung over and over again until its every syllable ached with nostalgia and sorrow.

MADELINE CORA RANDALL 1991 - 1991

Cora took another sip of her champagne and lifted her eyes toward the brewing late afternoon sky. It looked like the foggy insides of a big boiling pot. Had Madeline lived through those first fateful days of her existence, she would have turned thirty just last year. Nearly thirty at the time of her father's death.

What might that have looked like?

A thirtieth birthday party. Perhaps Madeline's husband, her children circled around a big table. Cora (a different version who'd gotten a whole lot better at baking) appeared with a beautifully iced birthday cake on which she'd placed ten flickering candles. Grandchildren. A son-in-law! A big house of laughter and love! Oh, how she would have embraced it with open arms.

It was best not to live in fantastical worlds, though. They reminded you of the grayness of your own. She forced her eyes open to stare yet again at the gravestones that marked both her husband and her infant daughter's deaths. Her stomach curdled with chill and champagne. Had she eaten anything? A piece of toast? A banana? Probably nothing. She couldn't remember.

Only once had Victor mentioned just what fun it might have been to have little Madeline in their community theater productions. It was almost a sure thing (in their minds, at least) that she would have been the belle of the ball, the featured little girl in everything from *Les Miserables* to *Annie*. She'd have started in tap and ballet at the age of four on top of acting and dictation lessons from her father and mother. Perhaps she'd have become a beauty queen contestant. "With that face and that talent and the way she carries herself, there's no doubt in my mind she'll win the pageant." Who said this in Cora's imagination? She wasn't entirely sure. But it seemed as true as anything at that moment.

"Everything Madeline touches turns to gold." She whispered this as though she spoke to Madeline's imaginary teachers, imaginary friends, and imaginary enemies. She sipped the red Solo cup till it was empty and reached for another drop of champagne just as a large raindrop slapped the side of her hand.

Her imagination had gotten the better of her again. And here was reality in the form of thick, wet snow ready to drag her back.

A flurry of wind and wet snowflakes splattered over her. There was a sudden rush to the left when one of the graveyard workers hustled toward her with an umbrella lifted. Cora hardly felt the severity of the weather as her hair started to become damp. She blinked up at the graveyard worker's tired-looking face as he toiled over her, protecting them both from the cold wetness.

"Oh goodness. Thank you." Cora swallowed and tried to smile sweetly. "Would you like some champagne?"

"What, lady?"

"Champagne! Do you want some?"

"I'm sober. Ten years."

"That's... that's incredible." Cora's eyes filled with tears. She now saw herself through this man's eyes— a tearful woman on the edge of her own sanity, celebrating her silly part in a community theater musical with the two people she loved the most. Neither of those people existed on this plane any longer. She was completely alone.

Cora stood on shaking legs, gathered her things, and followed the man's umbrella's shadow back toward the parking lot. Once she was safely seated in the front of her vehicle, the man raised a sturdy hand and then headed back for the shed, where the other graveyard workers continued to huddle beneath the overhang. The smoke from their cigarettes created a strange haze around the small building.

After another five minutes, Cora turned on her engine and drove the ten minutes back to her house in downtown Oak Bluffs, which she and Victor had purchased when they'd been late twentysomethings. Cora had been pregnant. The house had been a necessity for a future they hadn't been allowed.

But back at the house, Cora heard another ding from her phone, a sign that an email had come through.

It was from Lola, her new theater director.

Hello Miss Hannigan,

Thank you for gifting us with the depth of your talent. We'll have hard copies of the script for everyone at rehearsal tomorrow, but I wanted to send you a PDF version, just in case you want to get a head start. I'm a newbie at life "behind the scenes," and I'll need your help every step of the way. I know you're much more than a veteran of the stage. You're a true artist.

Looking forward to getting to know you better,
Lola

Chapter Eight

Rehearsals for the community theater production of *Annie* began on Monday, January tenth. Throughout the hours before the first meeting, which was slated to begin at four p.m. sharp, Lola sat at the kitchen table of the Sheridan House and outlined a specific schedule for the following six weeks of rehearsals. According to Greta, "perfection was out of the question," given the unprofessional nature of the troupe. That said, Lola felt they could inch toward refinement as long as they had a specific schedule, memorized their lines and music on time, and kept a general upbeat mood. To be a leader, Lola knew that she had to embody the emotion she wanted her team to feel.

"Lola! Lola!" Wes bustled in from the back porch, the ears of his hat flapping around behind him.

Lola whipped her head around so quickly that, in turn, she cracked her neck. Pain permeated at the base and along her shoulder as she cried out. "Ugh!" Her eyes clamped closed as she waited for the pain to slowly fade away. "Forty is really forty, isn't it?" she muttered to her father.

"Oh, honey. I hate it when that happens. Are you okay?" Wes sat at the kitchen table with her and removed his winter hat. Beneath, his white-gray hair was damp with sweat. Throughout the previous hour, he'd wandered around the outline of the two Frampton and Sheridan properties, watching for birds. Even now, his binoculars bounced against his chest in a friendly manner, reminding him to head back out.

"I'm fine. What did you want to tell me?" Lola asked. The pain remained a subtle scream in the back of her neck.

"I just saw that cardinal again," Wes informed her. "I wanted you to take a gander before he flew off."

"Oh gosh." Lola blinked down at the calendar she'd built for the next six weeks of rehearsals, which now looked like the savage writings of a madwoman. "Let's go." She jumped up, pushed her feet into winter boots, grabbed her coat, and headed out to the driveway. Wes was hot on her heels.

"He's flown off," Wes said, his voice heavy with disappointment. He lifted his binoculars and searched the tiptops of trees for some sign of the bright-red bird. "He's a tricky one."

Lola pushed her hands deeper into her pockets as she scanned the top of the trees. "He only likes you, Dad. You know that."

"And Kellan," Wes affirmed. "I miss that kid when he's off at school all day."

Lola dropped her head onto the chill of her father's shoulder and watched as the winter breeze curved through the tops of the pine trees, whipping them to and fro. There was nothing like the fresh air of a winter afternoon, sharp and simmering with the smell of pine.

"Maybe take a picture of him next time you see him," Lola suggested.

Wes's blue eyes glittered with thought. "I don't know. I get the sense that he wouldn't like that. He wouldn't like to be kept so still in a photograph, you know? So permanent."

A twittering of little birds rushed out from a tree farther out. Wes quickly grabbed his binoculars and put them in position. He then quietly inched his way slowly toward the birds, his footfalls as gentle as a predator's. Lola's heart swelled with love for this man, who witnessed such beauty on a day-to-day basis and felt the enormity of a small cardinal's heart.

The first week or so of rehearsals were, in a word, clumsy. Lola found that her best-laid plans were tossed out the window due to the nature of some of the younger children's talent and lack of experience. Even still, she and her worthy assistant directors flung themselves into their jobs with enthusiasm and optimism and refused to give in.

Naturally, Cora Randall's Miss Hannigan was a real sight to see. She tore into the role as though she was Al Pacino in *The Godfather* or Meryl Streep in anything she'd ever done. She mastered her song and dance numbers easily with the grace of a ballerina and frequently assisted with the stage direction and line memorization for other cast members.

Lola and Cora built up a wonderful rapport after only

a few days of rehearsals. Cora teased her gently, laughed at their joint mistakes, and also seemed to make Jenny, the little girl who'd nabbed the part of Annie, more comfortable on stage, despite her clear nerves.

"You really have to belt this note out, Jenny," Cora instructed the young girl, sitting cross-legged on the ground in front of her. "This last note is the final word we hear from the first act. We need to use your energy to get into the next act and continue to build the story. We're all counting on you."

Jenny puffed out her chest, then tore through her solo of "Tomorrow," after that, time and again, like her life depended on it. Each time afterward, Cora winked at her, showing her immense approval. After rehearsal, Cora frequently met with Lola, Audrey, and Amanda to discuss the weaknesses in their growing performance and what to attack next.

"She's the unofficial director of *Annie*," Lola informed Amanda and Audrey as Cora collected her coat and gloves.

"We'd be lost without her," Audrey agreed.

"But Jenny's a real Annie. That's for sure. We made the right choice," Amanda affirmed, referencing that they'd really struggled to decide who would play the titular character. The conversation about it had toiled long into the night.

"Good night, ladies." This was Hank, the man who'd nabbed the role of Daddy Warbucks. He marched past them with a big backpack over his shoulders and a thick wool hat over his ears. At sixty-two, he was the oldest person in the theater troupe and a newcomer on the Martha's Vineyard community theater scene. "See you tomorrow."

"Night, Hank!" Lola called as Hank disappeared through the back door, immediately after Cora.

"Do you know much about Hank?" Amanda asked as she wrapped a scarf around her neck.

"Not really," Lola replied. "He doesn't seem to talk much to the other actors."

"I think he's shy," Audrey added, pulling on her gloves.

"Well, he's certainly not shy about his performance," Amanda affirmed. "He gives it all on stage."

"I think that's part of being shy," Audrey pointed out. "In some contexts, you can pretend that's not who you really are. Like when you put on different clothes or play a fictional character."

"I think that's part of the reason Cora's a master at Miss Hannigan," Lola explained. "It's the perfect escape from her real life."

Amanda's and Audrey's faces grew soft and thoughtful as they wandered out toward the dark and chilly night. Lola gathered her elaborate notes from the day's rehearsal and followed them. Their drive back to the Sheridan House for dinner was a quiet one. It very much felt as though this production of *Annie* meant something different to each of them. It was difficult yet essential to imagine each character's complex reasons for taking on their specific roles.

* * *

On January twentieth, Jenny's Annie, orphans Rachel, Gail, Abby, and several other little girls from Oak Bluffs and Edgartown, along with Cora's Miss Hannigan, performed in the makeshift orphanage. It was nearly the end of the scheduled rehearsal, and the little girls were exhausted, dragging themselves through the song and dance and aching to go home for dinner. Rachel, Gail, and Abby, ever the troublemakers, burst into bouts of giggles as Lola attempted to instruct Jenny. Audrey scolded them playfully, saying she'd tell their Grandpa Trevor what monsters they were. This shut them up for a good while. Trevor Montgomery's anger was nothing to scoff at.

"Let's do it one more time," Lola instructed the actors before her. "And then we can all run on home and rest for the night."

Rhonda, the pianist, counted off the song. "A one. A two. A one, two, three..."

The little orphan girls and Miss Hannigan burst into song and dance right on time. Lola tapped her foot on the ground to keep time within herself as the girls scuttled across the stage. This time, perhaps because they'd been promised the chance to leave rehearsal, their faces remained bright and performative throughout. Miss Hannigan, naturally, was a burst of light, alternating between what seemed to be twelve different emotions at any given time.

When the song petered out, Lola, Audrey, and Amanda burst to their feet with triumph and clapped their hands wildly with excitement. Audrey placed two fingers in her mouth and whistled like a coach.

"That's what I'm talking about!" Lola cried. "Let's see everyone give a bow."

Together, the ten orphans and Cora bent halfway toward the ground and then rose, nearly collapsing with laughter. Cora's eyes were alight with joy. When the girls headed backstage to collect their things, Cora stepped toward Lola. This time, she hadn't any instructions or directions or suggestions.

Instead, she looked on the verge of tears.

Cora sat down at the edge of the stage so her legs dangled out in front of her. "Lola... That was such a wonderful rehearsal. Thank you for your commitment to our little troupe."

Lola's throat tightened. She told herself not to cry. "It's my pleasure," she told Cora.

"I learned from a bit of gossip that you're about to be married." Cora leaned against the stage.

"That's right." Lola's heart lifted. "My fiancé thinks I'm crazy for taking this on along with everything else. But it's when I feel most alive, I think."

"He must be a really special man," Cora returned, smiling.

"He is a very special person and right now, a bit of a brat. He's texting me, demanding pizza for dinner. He's been up since three-thirty, working on the freight lines with my brother-in-law, Scott. So I guess it stands to reason that he's starving."

Cora laughed good-naturedly. "No matter how good a man is, he can always be brought down by his stomach."

Lola tilted her head, burning with curiosity about this woman, about all she'd lost. She could practically feel what Cora yearned to say next.

"My husband would have loved this," Cora breathed finally as her eyes wandered around the room and then landed back on Lola. "He would have loved you as a director and he would have loved to joke with you and the little girls. I could see him playing either my brother or Daddy Warbucks— he would have been a killer Daddy Warbucks. You should have heard that man sing..."

Lola dropped her chin at the intensity of these emotions. "I so wish he was here with us now, Cora."

Cora drew her sleeve around her hand and wiped the length of it beneath her eye, collecting tears. Slowly, she pushed herself away from the stage, righting herself before adding, "He just loved the theater. It fills me with such regret that we weren't allowed more time on stage together. But I know he wouldn't want me to be anywhere else. Thank you, Lola. Thank you for directing this performance. He thought *Annie* was a silly little musical, but one with plenty of heart."

Cora turned and headed back into the darkness behind the stage. Hank was standing in the shadows, dressed in partial Daddy Warbucks' costuming, watching her. Cora hustled past him as he bowed his head, honoring her sorrow.

Chapter Nine

The following evening, Charlotte invited the Sheridan sisters to her home to go over the immense strategy she'd plotted for the upcoming Sheridan-Gasbarro wedding. Charlotte had told Lola once that she considered her career as a wedding planner to be like a chess game. She had full control over the pieces on the board, the caterers, the venues, even the bride and the groom. She just had to orchestrate when and how to move them around to maximize winning potential. "You really know how to take the romance out of weddings," Lola had teased, but at this, Charlotte's eyes became glossy as she'd said, "No. In fact, romance is the reason the game begins at all."

An hour after rehearsal finished for the week, the handsome photojournalist Everett opened the door to the home he and Charlotte had recently purchased. He peered out onto the snow-covered Lola, Christine, Susan, Amanda, and Audrey, together with babies Max and Mia and enough wine to get them through the chilly night. Everett's mischievous smile was one for the record books.

He beckoned them in and said, "I don't know what I did right to have the likes of you darken my door on this Friday night."

"Are they here?" Charlotte appeared in the doorway between the kitchen and the foyer, still in an apron that sported wisps of flour. Her smile was electric. She tore off the apron and hustled for Lola first before delivering hugs to the rest of the clan. "Claire should be here in a jiffy. The girls are all upstairs, as usual, although I have a hunch you've had enough of Rachel, Gail, and Abby for one week."

"They aren't exactly the most well-behaved of all our orphans," Lola teased. "But they bring a certain charm to set."

"I just hope you don't fire them," Charlotte told her. "What else would they do? Who knows what kind of trouble they'd get themselves into?" Her eyes were glistening, proof she was joking. She beckoned them into the living area, where she'd set up large charcuterie boards featuring juicy grapes, slabs of camembert, various meats, brie, crackers, dates and slices of cucumber and mixed nuts.

"The pizza will be out of the oven soon," Charlotte announced.

"Homemade dough?" Christine asked, impressed as she perched at the edge of the couch to bring the sleeping baby away from her chest.

"Nothing but the best from Charlotte," Everett affirmed.

"Well, you did move across the country for a reason," Charlotte teased.

"Yes, I did. The reason I moved here from LA was based on your cooking alone," Everett returned, rolling his eyes sarcastically. "I'll get the pizza out of the oven in a few minutes. You ladies have a lot to discuss. I'll let you get started."

Claire arrived several minutes later with a bountiful display of freshly-cut flowers and a big dollop of donut jelly on her otherwise perfectly-ironed button-down shirt. She laughed outright as she walked in, drawing attention to what she'd done.

"I was starving before I left work and crammed one of the Frosted Delights donuts into my mouth. This is what I get. Proof that I'm a slob."

"Come on. We're all foodies here. We get it," Audrey said. She quickly flipped through her purse and drew out a Tide-to-Go pen, which Claire thanked her for. "Max is almost one. Quick cleanup options are necessities at this point. Especially since I'm, you know... dating. Noah's found one too many spit-up stains on my T-shirts."

"But you said he also has them sometimes," Lola added. "Because of his little sister."

"Yes. I'm lucky to be dating someone just about as messy as me," Audrey agreed.

Charlotte disappeared for a moment to fetch a vase for the flowers. When she returned, Everett was hot on her heels with two large pizzas, fresh out of the oven and already sliced. Everett set the pizzas on a little table off to the right of the sofa to allow the women to serve themselves. As Claire slid the flowers into a vintage vase, Charlotte set up a large bulletin board, on which she'd positioned a number of facts about the approaching "big day."

"I've already booked the gorgeous Union Chapel for Sunday, February twenty-seventh," Charlotte said. "It's absolutely perfect for your number of guests. I almost wept thinking about you in your wedding dress and Tommy in a tuxedo, saying your vows there to one another."

"She really did!" Everett called from the next room.

"If Mom ever finds a wedding dress, that is..." Audrey teased.

"It's been crazy with rehearsals," Lola admitted as she grabbed a cracker.

"Oh, come on. You've had time. You told me you've tried on twenty-five different dresses," Christine countered. "You're just picky."

Lola laughed outright. It was unimaginable to her that they sat in this room discussing the intricacies of her own wedding. Lola Sheridan! Married?

"We'll start the ceremony at four-thirty and then depart for the reception afterward. I have three options for that..." Charlotte began.

"I want to have it at the Sunrise Cove," Lola interjected.

Charlotte blinked back at her, perplexed. "Are you sure you don't want to hear my ideas?"

"It's... it's my family's inn," Lola tried to explain, her smile faltering. "It's where my mother and father basically raised us. It's one of the reasons I came back and ultimately met Tommy in the first place. It means so much to me. I can't imagine it not being a part of the service."

Susan arched her brow and added, "I suppose your guest list isn't as big as mine and Scott's was. It could work."

"And I think it would make Dad really happy," Lola added, her voice softening. "And I know that he's felt so good lately. He's seemed so chipper. But I'm reminded several times a week that we don't fully know the nature of his disease. We don't really know how—"

"How much longer we have with him," Susan finished, eyeing the floor. "I think about it, too."

"All right. Well. It sounds like we're all in agreement, then," Charlotte said, her voice returning to chipper brightness. "If the Bistro's all right with you, then it'll have to do. We'll have it looking like a magical fairy tale in no time. Make it extra special."

"That's right. Plenty of flowers," Claire winked before adding. "I was thinking French Tulips. Holly. Jasmine. Orchids... Winter flowers that exude beauty and light."

"You're a true artist, Claire," Lola smiled at her cousin.

Charlotte continued with her ideas, discussing her contacts in the wedding industry, and displaying some of her favorite wedding photographers, making it easy for Lola to make quick decisions.

"I never imagined finalizing my wedding would seem so seamless," Lola said, genuinely flabbergasted.

From the next room, Everett called, "It's definitely not as easy as Charlotte makes it look."

Lola giggled. "I think you have a hype man in the next room."

"He's too good to me," Charlotte replied as a blush crept up her cheeks. "But in all honesty, you told me to keep it simple, so I kept it simple."

"It took enough time to get these two to the altar," Susan offered with a shrug. "We don't want to scare them away."

Lola dropped her head back against the headrest of the coach as her stomach swelled with pizza and wine.

"Imagine if I really leaned into all the wedding tropes. Four hundred guests with a huge Barbie-style wedding dress with little flower girls running around. Tommy would take one look at it and run off on his sailboat for the rest of his life."

"We'd be like, 'Where's Tommy?' And the answer would be, 'Somewhere near South America already,'" Audrey joked as she lifted a sleeping Max from her lap and headed off for his baby carrier, where she positioned him gently so he could continue through his sleep unperturbed.

"Naw. I've been around a lot of couples," Charlotte affirmed. "The way Tommy looks at you... I don't see that with every couple. It's something special. I really mean that."

"Gosh, I think I'm going to cry." Susan bent her head low and dabbed the edge of her eye with her sleeve, blotting her tears away.

"Pull it together, sis," Lola said, shifting her weight to place her head on Susan's shoulder beside her on Charlotte's couch.

Amanda, seated on the floor at her mother's feet, tried to explain. "It's been a hard day at work. One of our clients had an all-out meltdown in the foyer. Bruce had to take him out. Mom took the brunt of his anger." Amanda then lifted a hand to her mother's and gently wrapped her fingers around her wrist.

"But all that doesn't matter, now," Susan affirmed, sniffling as she lifted her chin. "Because I'm here planning my little sister's wedding to the love of her life. It's like a dream come true."

"Let the world know that Susan Sheridan's gone full sap on us," Christine teased as she joined Lola and Susan on the couch and struggled to wrap her arms around the both of them.

"Don't you dare tell anyone," Susan cried. "It could ruin my cred as a criminal lawyer."

With the plans relatively finalized, the flowers decided upon, the photographer emailed to confirm, and even the four-course meal a done-deal, the Sheridan and Montgomery girls found themselves with nothing but a whole night of gossip, wine, snacks, and conversation before them. It was a relief, Lola thought, not to consider the weight of the approaching performance of the musical theater troupe, nor the chaos of the wedding festivities, and just lean into the beautiful rhythm of the voices she adored the most in the world.

Soon after, Gail, Rachel, and Abby hopped down the steps to show off their new dance, which they'd apparently been upstairs rehearsing for the previous three hours. At sixteen, the girls danced along the edge of youthful silliness and womanhood, not fully comprehending the weight of their approaching powers. When Rachel misstepped during the dance, she burst into childish giggles and fell to the floor, and Gail and Abby joined her, laughing outright.

"All right, that's it," Charlotte cried, half-joking, half-serious. "The three of you are wound up on chocolate bars. I can feel it."

"Mom..." Rachel cried as tears brewed in her eyes.

"No, no. Do it again," Lola said as she scampered to her feet. "Audrey? You want to join me?"

"You honestly think you can learn the dance?" Abby asked, with the jagged sass of a teenage girl.

"Try me," Lola shot, inching her smile from ear to ear.

Over the next thirty-five minutes, a nearly married woman of forty, her twenty-year-old daughter, and her cousins' daughters traced through the frantic motions of a silly dance, cackling as they made mistakes and taking frequent pauses for snacks and pizza. Lola wasn't sure what made her feel so youthful and rejuvenated. She marveled that it was simply the power of Tommy's love and the life they'd built together. She marveled at the strength it had given her to become better, brighter, more alive (even if, admittedly, it didn't make her a better dancer).

Chapter Ten

On the final Saturday of the first month of the new year, the entirety of Martha's Vineyard awoke to a sparkling winter wonderland. Lola blinked through the sterling light of morning, Tommy's powerful arm wrapped over her stomach, and took in the heaviness of the silence in their cabin, tucked deep within the forest and now covered in a foot and a half of snow. Tommy remained asleep, his face soft as his head lay adorably against his pillow. Lola lifted her head the slightest bit to catch the time, which blared out from the red alarm clock on the side table. It was just past nine in the morning, over five hours later than Lola and Tommy ordinarily slept. It was a perfect luxury.

Lola tried to go back to sleep, to join Tommy back in the soft darkness of unconsciousness, but unfortunately, her body nagged for the bathroom. Slowly, she eased out from under Tommy's arm and tiptoed to the bathroom in the hallway, where she took in her mirror reflection, a sleepy-eyed Lola with bright porcelain skin and hints of crow's feet— proof of the forty years she'd walked on earth.

Once in the kitchen, Lola brewed a pot of coffee and peeked out the back door to investigate the snow situation. As Lola had spent the previous evening at the Sheridan House playing cards with Grandpa Wes, Audrey, Noah, and Amanda, she hadn't given a thought to any approaching weather. When snow was a surprise like this, it reminded Lola of her childhood. Back then, a blanket of snow had meant the world to her. It had felt like a delicious gift from God himself.

As the coffee pot bubbled and spat, Tommy appeared in the doorway of the kitchen, still shirtless, with baggy flannel pants floating around his muscular legs. His black hair was disheveled, hair sticking up every which way. Lola took two strides toward him before falling into his embrace. She then pressed her cheek against the soft pillow of his chest hair. Was it possible to tell someone you loved them too often? She held on to the silence until Tommy laughed good-naturedly and lifted her off the ground and into him.

"We got quite a snowfall last night," he said, his grin widening.

"Looks like we're trapped in this cabin all alone."

"Oh no. Trapped with you? What have I done to deserve this?" Tommy demanded.

"It's awful, isn't it?" She cocked her top lip, trying to make a nasty face.

Tommy kissed her gently, then harder, before placing her delicately back on the floor. Lola whipped back around to pour them two mugs of coffee and placed two pieces of bread in the toaster. It was marvelous to be there, just the two of them, without rehearsals to run off to or freight lines to sail. Perhaps this was her version of happily ever after.

As Lola and Tommy settled into the breakfast nook with toast and coffee, Audrey sent a photograph of herself and Amanda, already knee-deep in the snow and erupting with laughter. Lola smiled inwardly and wrote back.

LOLA: You girls are always up to no good.

Another photo came in of Max, dressed in thick layers with little mittens on his hands. He touched the snow delicately as though he didn't trust it. His blue eyes caught the sparkling sunlight that reflected off the snow.

Lola showed the photograph to Tommy, who answered with an appreciative, "He's an islander through and through, isn't he?"

Lola and Tommy inched themselves through the rest of the morning, frequently falling into one another's arms and often talking about just getting back in bed and avoiding all tasks for the day ahead. As the clock hinted toward noon, Tommy suggested they take the snowmobiles out for a drive through the woods, perhaps all the way to the sea.

"I can't keep you landlocked for even a day, can I?" Lola teased gently as she pulled on a turtleneck, a sweatshirt, and then an additional layer, all of which would go under her winter coat.

"It's the only way I know how to live," Tommy told her.

Lola and Tommy had only snowmobiled together a handful of times the previous winter, especially as Tommy hadn't been on the island for very much of it. Lola knew, however, that Tommy was a worthy snowmobiler, someone she could trust easily to forge a path forward. Wes Sheridan himself had taught Lola the ins and outs of the snowmobile culture throughout her teenage years— after Susan had already left the island and Christine was usually upstairs listening to Nirvana CDs and lamenting the world. Although Lola and her father hadn't seen eye-to-eye until very recently, she had fond memories of those beautiful winter days, whizzing atop the snow as the softness of it rained on either side of her, projected back.

Lola fell into the daydream of the early afternoon. They whipped easily through the trees, their bodies leaned forward, and their machines powerful and precise. Much of the island wouldn't be plowed in time for anyone outside the bigger towns to get anywhere. Several other snowmobilers were out and about, joyfully cutting around the snow-topped island. Lola waved to several passers-by, each of whom wore their Skidoo outfits, along with helmets that protected them from the elements and made them generally unrecognizable until they stopped and lifted their visors.

Eventually, Tommy led them to the Aquinnah Cliff-side Overlook Hotel, where Lola's cousin Kelli and her new boyfriend developer had ceased work over the previous few weeks due to winter conditions. They parked the snowmobiles in the makeshift parking lot, which would soon become a parking lot filled with antique vehicles, Porsches, Lamborghinis, and BMWs, the vehicles of the wealthy folks who would come to darken the doors of this once-great and soon-to-be-great-again hotel.

"It's hard to imagine the future, isn't it?" Lola breathed as she walked toward the cliff's edge. "When the island takes on winter, it's like summer never happened at all."

"That hotel will be just about the ritziest place on this island, won't it?" Tommy scrunched his nose as he inspected the outline of the place, which mostly covered in snow.

Lola leaned her head on his chest and peered up at it. "You know the old story. That my grandfather met my grandmother there, but she was married to a terrible man."

"And your grandfather sold the hotel to her husband just before he found out about the affair," Tommy recited.

"In the middle of a hurricane!"

"You love the old romance of this place, don't you?" Tommy teased.

"How could I not?" Lola returned, her throat tightening. "Call me a sap, but it's my family's history. And it's larger than life."

Tommy studied her, his brow furrowed. "Did I ever tell you about the story of how my mother met my father?"

"No..." Lola's eyes widened. "I didn't think you even knew."

"My mother told me," Tommy began gently. His eyes turned toward the horizon line, a wide-open Atlantic Ocean, which the wind toiled against, drawing large waves toward the sky. "She was traveling through Italy, which I suppose you know, and she was nearing the end of her trip. She was short on funds but managed to find a little bed and breakfast in Rome."

"What is it about the hospitality industry?" Lola asked. "It seems like that's where all stories begin and end."

"Yes, well. In this particular story, my mother awoke in the middle of the night to a fire. The entire bed and breakfast had gone up in flames. Something was wrong with the oven, I believe, although I'm not entirely sure."

"Oh my gosh."

"She ran to the staircase, but the smoke was too intense. She couldn't get through. So she returned to her bedroom and found that the house had a little escape ladder out beside the window. As she pulled open the bedroom window to escape, she found that a man had crawled up to save her. He didn't speak a word of English, but he beckoned for my mother to take the ladder up above him and crawl down so that he could guide her, catching her if she fell. My mother was terrified of heights and of water and most certainly, of falling. But inch by inch, my father guided my mother down that ladder back to the ground below. And then, almost immediately, she fainted."

Lola shrieked. "Evelyn! I had no idea."

"Yes, well. He took her back to his mother's house, and together, the two of them nursed her back to health, refusing to allow her back on her journey. By the week's end, my father had charmed her so much that she called it a version of Stockholm syndrome."

"Roman syndrome," Lola countered. "With all that pasta, I don't know how you could resist."

"Yes," Tommy agreed, smiling. "My mother said there were red flags about him left and right. That he flirted with everyone and probably had some other lovers at the time that they met. But she couldn't bear it when it came time for her to return home. They stayed up throughout the night talking, and then my father told my mother he wouldn't let her go. Not unless she allowed him to come along with her."

"Wow..." Lola breathed. "That's so romantic."

Tommy shrugged flippantly as his eyes hardened. "It is. It's a beautiful, incredibly romantic Italian story. But you see... this story is the reason that I've never been able to trust anything or anyone. How could my father say such beautiful things to my mother and then leave her like that? Leave her with a little boy who hardly knew anything at all? How could you build such a story with someone and then completely retreat without looking back?"

Lola recognized the weight of Tommy's sorrow— the sinister reason he'd never believed in the power of love or marriage. Unfortunately, he had this ingrained into him at such a young age.

Lola placed her hands across Tommy's chest and gazed into his eyes, which reflected the damage of his youth.

"Stories are never enough, Tommy," she whispered. "The sheer fact that my grandparents met during a hurricane when my grandmother was married to someone else... doesn't make their love a success. For me, their love was a success because they had mornings like the morning we just had. They woke up next to one another and chose to talk and laugh and experience the world together. They woke up every day and chose love."

Tommy bowed his head gently and closed his eyes. Lola could almost feel the thumping of his heart beneath the layers of his thick outfit.

"I've never heard someone explain it like that before," Tommy whispered. "But I should have known from the moment I met you that you'd shift my perspective."

A dramatic chirp erupted above them. Lola lifted her head to catch the flash of a bright-red cardinal overhead. It landed on a long, skinny branch of a nearby tree and seemed to blink down at her expectantly.

"Look at him. He looks so perfect against the snow," Lola murmured.

But before Tommy could turn his head back to catch sight of him, the little cardinal swept out from the trees and headed back toward the inner part of the island, where he belonged.

Chapter Eleven

Lola Sheridan's Aunt Willa hovered on the outskirts of several different auditorium rehearsals throughout late January and early February. The beautiful yet tired-looking woman tapped her foot along with each musical number, mouthed along to the actors' lines, and took diligent notes throughout. Cora burned with curiosity regarding this woman. Didn't she have anything better to do than watch a community theater troupe rehearse? And what on earth did she scribble on that notepad of hers?

After Cora had a brief pow-wow with Lola regarding the afternoon's rehearsal on the first Tuesday of February, Cora watched, cat-eyed, as Willa gathered her things and slipped on her coat. Audrey Sheridan said something to Willa, something like, "We need to come by and check out your new apartment soon!" To this, Willa said simply, "Oh, it's not much. Just a couple of rooms to call my own."

Cora hadn't made a real friend in what seemed like twenty-five years. Victor had been her constant throughout adulthood, the only person she needed to get her through dark, chilly nights and everyday anxiety. Willa seemed a few years older than her, but not much, and she seemed to echo back the same sort of loneliness that Cora felt day in, day out. Perhaps this was why Cora sped up to walk alongside her. Perhaps this was why she heard herself ask, "Where is it you've moved?"

Willa tilted her head, her face glowing with curiosity. "Miss Hannigan! Hello!"

Cora laughed outright, surprised at Willa's genuine gladness. "Please, call me Cora."

"Oh goodness me. I'm terribly embarrassed." Willa placed a hand on her heart and stumbled to a stop. "I've just watched you on that stage the past three weeks or so and thought to myself, 'What a talented woman.' You've become a celebrity in my book, is all. It's like Jennifer Aniston herself just walked up to me to say hello."

"You flatter me."

"It's silly, I know." Willa drew a dark strand behind her ear as her brows stitched together. This motion showed a wedding ring on her fourth finger. "Oh, how rude of me. I should answer your question. I've moved to a little apartment in downtown Oak Bluffs. I never imagined myself in an apartment, really, but it's quaint. And it's lovely not to have to do yard maintenance."

But where was the husband? Who had given her that ring? Cora ached with curiosity. She ached to know a story that wasn't her own.

"Are you from Oak Bluffs originally?" Cora asked.

"I am," Willa told her. "But my parents moved off the island when I was a little girl."

"I suppose that's why I don't know who you are,"

Cora replied. "Everyone knows everyone else around here— especially around our age."

Willa nodded as the color drained from her cheeks. Cora's heart quickened. What was the script for making a new friend? Had she already messed it up?

"Listen," Cora began. "There's a winter festival in downtown Oak Bluffs with a few small kiosks of mulled wine and various foods with coffee and sweets. I thought that since we're both headed downtown anyway, would you like to grab a cup of mulled wine with me?"

Willa's eyes widened with hesitation. "Are you sure about that?" She chuckled, then added, "I've been something of a mess the past few months. I'm sure you've heard about it."

Cora shook her head. "On the contrary, I can't imagine that anyone could be viewed as a bigger mess than me."

Willa processed this information slowly as though she tried to see it from all angles.

"I'll probably grab a mulled wine whether you join me or not," Cora tried a final time. "But I'd love the company."

"Good evening, ladies!" Lola, Amanda, and Audrey hurried past, waving before they disappeared into the darkness of the back hallway. Both Willa and Cora watched them depart in silence.

"I wish I could bottle their energy sometimes," Willa breathed. "They burn so brightly."

"Your sister was their mother?"

"Anna. Yes." Willa dropped her gaze to the floor and seemed to draw deeper into herself.

Cora cursed herself for bringing up such a wretched

memory. "I'm terribly sorry. Really. I promise, if we head out for mulled wine, I won't say a single bad thing."

Willa's smile was genuine yet sorrowful. "Promising that will get you into heaps of trouble, I imagine."

Cora laughed good-naturedly. "You have me pegged, don't you?"

The two women struck out from the auditorium, bundled up in coats and walking carefully across the shoveled sidewalk. Silence hung heavy between them. Cora knew the weight of this was on her shoulders, that she'd requested this fresh conversation due to general fear about returning home for another night alone.

"When did you get started in musical theater?" Willa finally asked, drawing them out from the depths of their silence.

"Oh goodness. I was just a little girl." Cora swallowed as waves of memories crashed over her. "I fell in love with tap dance and ballet and singing myself silly. My mother nearly tore my head off."

They stopped at a traffic light, shifting their weight. Willa's eyes flashed toward hers as she asked, "Lola mentioned your husband. I'm terribly sorry."

Cora was surprised at the sincerity that lurked beneath Willa's words. It was true what she'd sensed. Willa's sorrow was a mountain, just like her own.

"Thank you," Cora breathed. "He would have loved working with Lola. He always had such energy when it came time for the musical. He always woke up early, exercised, and then worked until rehearsal while banging out musical number after musical number. I told him he was like the Energizer Bunny."

They made their way toward downtown as Willa asked a series of questions about Cora and Victor's time in the theater troupe and her favorite roles that they'd taken on. Very soon, they neared the little winter market and waited in a line of five for two mugs of mulled wine and a little bag of powdered donuts. They then shifted off to the side and perched on a downtown park bench with the donut baggy between them, their mugs steaming.

Was this what it was like to have a friend? Cora hadn't done anything like this with anyone but Victor... ever? Cora sipped her hot wine. The spices simmered across her tongue. In the distance, the high school choir sang a selection of winter-themed songs like "Let it Snow! Let it Snow! Let it Snow!"

"I lost my husband, too," Willa confessed finally, her voice barely audible.

"I saw the ring on your finger," Cora returned. "I wasn't sure how to bring it up."

Willa nodded. "I remember being a younger woman, hearing stories about widows. Reading about the crippling loneliness. Nobody ever tells you what it's really like."

"How would you describe it? I've struggled to put it into words."

Willa considered this for a moment. She lifted a powdered donut toward the soft light emanating from a nearby streetlamp. "It's like every day tramples over you. You're battered, bruised, and terrified to keep going because you know that every day will be the same. Just as painful and just as suffocating. Then you realize that you have to do something menial like buy milk or pay your bills. You ask yourself, 'Why me?' And there's no answer, so you just keep going."

A tear rolled down Cora's left cheek. She swiped it away before it froze against her cheek. "Why me? I think that all the time. He was so young."

"Mine too."

Cora shuddered inwardly, then lifted her mug of wine toward Willa's. "To the loves of our lives. How blessed we were to have had them for as long as we did."

"Terribly blessed," Willa agreed as she clicked her mug against Cora's.

Willa then went on to tell Cora about the events that had transpired after her husband's death. She'd developed psychosis and essentially forgotten who she was, who her husband was. She'd arrived on Martha's Vineyard searching for her long-lost sister and had fallen into the arms of the Sheridan clan.

"They've been such a Godsend," Willa finished. "They're always eager to help out wherever they can— eager to sit with me and talk to me about everything and anything. The younger one, Audrey Sheridan, she's the one who discovered the truth of my husband's death, believe it or not. I can hardly believe it all happened the way it did. But now, the doctor says my medication is working well; I have full control over my thoughts. Now, as sad as it sounds, all I have to do is deal with my own sorrow. And that will be a lifelong journey."

Cora bowed her head. "After my husband's death, the funeral home sent me information about widows' groups. It's meetings for women to gather around and talk about their feelings. The thought disgusted me. Why should I allow anyone to hear my thoughts about my husband? They're private. Yet here with you now, I feel a relief that

I haven't experienced since... well. Since everything happened."

Willa folded a hand over Cora's and made eye contact with her. Sometimes, words weren't enough. Just as she opened her lips to attempt some sort of dialogue, anything to get them through the sharpness of their sorrow, a name came out through the little winter festival crowd.

"Cora? Cora!"

Cora's eyes lifted in surprise. There, coming out of the crowd of Oak Bluffs residents, was Hank, the man who played Daddy Warbucks in their production of *Annie*. His smile was electric, friendly in a way that suggested they hadn't seen one another in quite some time, rather than only about forty-five minutes.

"Hi, Hank." Cora stood on shivering legs to greet him.

He drew closer. He walked with overzealous energy, like a teenager about to ask a young woman on a date. When he neared them, he lifted his mulled wine in greeting and said, "You were a wonder at rehearsal today, Miss Hannigan. I told my daughter on the phone last night that you were meant for Broadway or something like it. The kind of talent you don't normally find in community theater."

"Oh, I don't know about that."

"It's true," Willa interjected as she, too, rose from the bench. "I've been amazed at her performance and yours, Daddy Warbucks. The way you dance around that stage with little Annie... It almost breaks my heart."

"It's keeping me young," Hank beamed. "And I have to push myself to keep up with my costars."

Cora had never said much more than a few real, unscripted words to Hank. She tried to drum up some sort of interest in him, in his life. After all, he was a person in her community theater troupe. It was best to show a vested interest in those around you, wasn't it?

"I, um. I suppose you've had quite a career in community theater?"

"I did quite a bit in New Jersey," he explained. "I tried to make my daughter fall in love with it, but she chose a very different path. She always thought it was a little silly to play pretend on stage. For me, playing pretend was the only way I could get through real life."

Cora's false smile faded slightly. Right before her eyes, Hank began to form into a full, three-dimensional person. She wasn't accustomed to such honest conversations, especially not all in one night.

"I know exactly what you mean," Cora murmured.

An expectant silence brewed between them. Cora suddenly felt as though Hank could see all the way through her. She swallowed another gulp of mulled wine while the high school choir began to sing an a cappella version of "That's Life" by Frank Sinatra in the distance.

"Well, I hope you ladies have a beautiful evening," Hank said finally. "I'm headed off to meet a friend. But I'll see you at rehearsals tomorrow?"

"Sure thing," Cora replied. "Thanks for saying hello."

Hank disappeared through the crowd as Willa and Cora returned to the bench. Cora's legs jumped beneath her as Hank's words swirled through her mind.

"So..." Willa began, her words almost playful. "How long has that man been in love with you?"

Cora's jaw dropped with surprise. "What? He's not in love with me. We've hardly ever spoken before."

Willa shrugged. "I don't know much about the world any longer, Cora. But I do know love when I see it. And that man, my dear, is in love. With. You. I guess you don't feel the same?"

"I don't, no," Cora returned. "I don't know that I could ever feel that way about anyone else. The concept of marrying again after all that..."

"I know," Willa agreed. "It seems crazy to build yourself up if only to hurt yourself again and again."

"It really does," Cora breathed. "No point to it. No point at all."

Chapter Twelve

ola often scoffed at women who said, "My wedding dress picked me rather than the other way around." That was until she experienced what she could only refer to later as "divine wedding dress intervention" in the form of a quick trip to Boston with Tommy to help him out with his mother's house.

For hours on end, she sat in Evelyn Ellis's study and pored through documents, reading fine prints, studying old photographs, and generally getting dust and grime all over herself. Regardless of how organized people were, regardless of what kind of stickler they were about cleanliness, it seemed that time still had its way with things like thirty-year-old manila envelopes.

Tommy groaned around four in the afternoon, stood to his feet, then walked toward the window with his hands on his hips. Lola joined him, gently rubbing the top of his back, feeling all the tension come off his muscles. This was the work of a wife, she knew. She saw the bad, good, and even in-between parts. She saw it all, and she knew it well. She was grateful for it.

"Why don't I pick us up some sandwiches from that place you like?" Lola breathed the words and kissed him gently on the arm, just about as high as her lips could reach. "We forgot to eat lunch. I'm sure you're starving."

"I don't know. I can't think about food."

"I'll go grab some sandwiches and some snacks," Lola affirmed. "And maybe some alcohol. We can work a couple more hours and then crash for the night. You said the freight needs you again in the morning?"

Tommy nodded. "Yes. I should be there around four."

"Not a problem," Lola said. "I can take the ferry back to Oak Bluffs and have Audrey pick me up. She and Max are normally awake around six anyway."

Tommy turned to meet her eyes. He looked disgruntled and obstinate, like a little kid on the verge of a meltdown. "Thank you, Lola." He grabbed her hand and brought it to his lips, where he kissed it gently. "Thank you for all you've done for me. I couldn't have done this without you."

Lola stepped out into the fourteen-degree Sunday afternoon and buttoned her coat up to her chin. Tommy's truck keys jangled in her right hand as she went. Tommy allowing her to drive his truck was a rare thing, so she was extra cautious as she drifted out from the driveway and crept down the side street to the main road. Her hands sat at ten and two, and she lifted herself upright, alert, watching every little dog walker and every vehicle half poised at a stop sign.

Tommy's favorite sandwich place was located on Marion and belonged to a man called Roy. As luck would have it, there was a fifteen-minute parking spot located just two stores down. Despite the massive nature of

Tommy's truck, Lola managed to parallel park like an expert, so much so that she texted Christine and Susan about it (like the little snotty younger sister she was).

> LOLA: Check it out! I parallel parked this monster truck like a master!

Susan wrote back almost immediately.

> SUSAN: I wouldn't risk my life driving Scott's or Tommy's trucks. You're brave.

> CHRISTINE: Sorry, are you looking for compliments? I haven't slept in twenty hours. How's that for deserving compliments?

Lola grinned inwardly and wrote back.

> LOLA: Sorry, Mama. You're a queen. When you look back at these times in twenty years, you'll be so thankful for them.

> CHRISTINE: Yeah. Right.

Lola locked the truck and headed off to Roy's Cold Cuts, where she ordered a meatball parmesan sandwich for Tommy and a big cheese pizza for herself (which she would ultimately share with Tommy). The teenager behind the counter told her it would be ten minutes. The place was stocked with other folks, hungry for their over-stuffed sandwiches. Lola stepped outside, suddenly anxious and yearning for that frigid air.

Outside, Lola inspected cozy Marion Street, a world of Boston that she hadn't frequented during her twenty years as a resident. She made her way this way, then that, biding her time, considering the upcoming week of rehearsals. It was now February ninth, which gave them very little time before their first performance— and just about as little time before her wedding. Over the previous week, the performers had truly come into their own, flinging themselves into their characters and memorizing their lines with incredible ease. Little "Annie" had had a single mistake on Friday afternoon, which had resulted in her bursting into tears for ten minutes straight. Cora had pulled her aside and whispered something in her ear— something that forced the girl's chin back up and her eyes to dry. "I won't do that again," Jenny, the little girl, recited to Lola back on stage. Lola's heart had shattered.

"Honey, we all have feelings we don't know what to do with," Lola had told her. "That's why we're here at the theater."

Jenny's lower lip had bubbled around for another few seconds before she regrouped and forced herself through another round of "Tomorrow," the song the character of Annie seemed to return to whenever she felt especially low.

Lola's eyes were half glazed when she lifted them toward the shop window next to Roy's Cold Cuts. It was a vintage place, adorable and teensy, with only about fifteen dresses from various fashion seasons hanging within. One, in particular, caught Lola's eye. It was an off-off white dress, bohemian in style and very chic, with a low-cut front, an empire waist, sleeves draped halfway down the upper arms, and flowing fabric cascading to the ground. Lola stopped short on the sidewalk as a Boston snowflake fluttered across her cheeks.

Before she knew what she'd done, Lola burst through

the shop door and rushed toward the gorgeous dress. She was speechless as she stood before it, as though the dress itself had beckoned her, stating this was it. This was everything she'd ever needed.

"Can I help you?" a young woman behind the counter asked.

"I, um. I just." Lola, a journalist who had a way with language, had never felt so speechless. "I'm terribly sorry, but could I please try this dress on?"

Within the next ten minutes, Lola walked out of the vintage boutique with the dress. It had been sewed in the seventies and worn by only one other woman before her. The woman had lived a long and healthy life alongside her husband until her untimely death at the age of seventy when her beautiful daughters (all three who looked "rather like Lola," the woman said) had brought the wedding dress to this very vintage boutique. Their hope, they explained, was that someone would get as much love from wearing this dress as their mother had.

Lola placed the gorgeous dress in the back of the truck, then positioned the truck's top over it, protecting the gorgeous beauty from the elements. When she sat back in the vehicle, completely breathless, she had a sudden lurch of fear. She'd forgotten something. Hadn't she? But what was it?

On command, a text message came in from Tommy.

> TOMMY: Hey! Did you get the
> sandwiches?

Lola laughed aloud as she leaped back out to pick up her pizza and meatball sub. Just as she walked through the rickety glass door, the teenager behind the counter called her name. She paid and then fled, armed with everything she needed for her brand-new life.

"A wife," she whispered as she drove Tommy's enormous truck back home. She would become a wife. And this was the very dress she would do it in. It was as though it had been waiting for her— waiting for her to turn forty after years of experience and years of heartache.

After the following Friday night's rehearsal, Lola, Amanda, and Audrey drove back to Susan's place for a Sheridan family dinner. Once they fell into the beautiful warmth of Susan's place, the rhythm of a traditional Sheridan family dinner began. Grandpa Wes prattled on about the birds he'd spotted that afternoon on his walk with Kellan; Aunt Willa discussed her recent friendship with Cora, their "Miss Hannigan," and how the two of them had gone shopping the previous afternoon, prior to Cora's rehearsal. Amanda blushed as she talked about her and Sam's recent date to an Edgartown wine bar, where he'd shown off his wine knowledge so much that the two had had to take a taxi home. Meanwhile, Susan rushed in and out, tending to everyone's glasses, asking questions and generally looking stressed out but grateful to have so many people to care for. This was Susan's way.

"Mom has an announcement," Audrey piped up as Susan fled back to the kitchen to check on the chicken.

"Oh, honey. It's not a big deal," Lola returned.

"It is! I never imagined you'd actually do it!" Audrey cried.

Lola rolled her eyes back as Amanda demanded, "What is she talking about?"

"I found my wedding dress," Lola confessed with finality.

"Lola!" All the color drained from Christine's cheeks. Susan blasted back out from the kitchen, her face echoing her shock. Naturally, with family, no matter what you did, you were bound to disappoint someone.

"Girls, you know me," Lola told them pointedly. "I had to do this by myself."

Susan and Christine exchanged glances. There was a strained awkwardness among them. In the distance came the sound of a massive truck creeping up over the rocks of the driveway. It was Tommy.

But as Lola crept to her feet, suddenly little Max, at nearly one year old, yanked himself up with the side of the armchair, and with a mighty yelp, he took several steps forward. Audrey popped forward to grab his hands and hold him aloft, right before he fell back onto his diaper. Everyone was silent with shock until Audrey burst into tears, dropped to her knees, and wrapped her arms around her little boy.

"His first steps!" Audrey cried. "I thought they were coming soon, but he knew just when to accomplish that task. He wanted to save his grandma from retribution."

"He's so big and strong!" Lola fell beside them and kissed her grandson warmly on the cheek as he giggled with pleasure. It was clear he knew he'd done a swell job. Perhaps in his mind, he just wanted to make fun of adults all around him for what they did all the time.

"Hello?" Tommy called from the mudroom as he kicked off his boots.

"Tommy! Come quick!" Lola called.

Tommy appeared to find the Sheridan family in the midst of a celebration. Audrey held on to a bouncing Max as Lola clapped her hands joyously. Amanda raised the volume of the music and then brought Grandpa Wes to his feet for a little dance. Grandpa Wes twirled her back and forth like a classic ballroom dancer, his motions simplistic and sure, as though he'd learned these skills years before.

"He just took his first steps!" Lola informed Tommy as she rose to kiss him on the lips.

"Is that right?" Tommy turned to grin down at little Max. "That's one first step for man, isn't it, little Max?"

"He's not quite walking on the moon yet," Audrey explained, her smile enormous. "Give him a few more years."

Over the following joyous hours, all the Sheridans ate chicken parmesan, played music, swapped stories, and danced in the living room. They drank several bottles of wine, cracked several pints of beer, and celebrated this particularly dark and chilly night in the middle of February, knowing that it was essential to uphold all special moments together, as there were no guarantees in life. This was it. They had to live every moment for the present.

That night, Tommy drove Lola back to the cabin they called home. When they stepped out into the blissful night, Lola lifted her eyes toward the sky and spotted a smattering of stars. They seemed extra-illuminated that evening, as though they sparkled down, knowingly blessing Lola, Audrey, Max, and Tommy and all the rest of their ever-growing family.

"I can't believe I get to grow old with you," Lola murmured suddenly, drawing her eyes toward Tommy's as they entered their cabin arm in arm.

Tommy chuckled. "I know it's just the wine talking, but I feel the same about you."

"Just the wine talking, huh?" Lola teased him, placing her elbow at the bottom of his belly and pushing gently.

Tommy drew the house keys from his pocket, unlocked the door, then bent to kiss her gently. "Don't push your luck, Little Sheridan," he said to her softly.

Back inside, Lola told Tommy about the following week of rehearsals— that suddenly, everything felt like it was heading forward in fast motion, and she couldn't catch herself.

"The costumes have almost been finalized," she explained. "And the girls look so cute in their little outfits. Daddy Warbucks refuses to shave his head, but we've found a little bald cap for him, which he says is uncomfortable, but it'll do."

Tommy looked at her, captivated. "You look like you're walking on air," he finally said.

"I feel like I am," she told him quietly. "I've never given back to my community like this. It's been one of the most rewarding experiences of my life."

"Do you think you'll keep doing it?" Tommy asked.

Lola burst out laughing. "No! No. I mean, no." She brushed a tear of exhaustion from her cheek and shrugged. "I love it, but I'll love when it's over, too, and I can just pass out in your arms every afternoon and watch the world go by."

"Are those your wedding vows?" Tommy teased.

"Just about," Lola returned. "I hope you don't think that just because I'm a writer, I'll have the world's best vows."

"Never," Tommy told her. "I would never think that."

Lola whacked him playfully, kissed him again, and

then headed back to the bathroom, where she scrubbed her forty-year-old face, donned her night creams, and prepared for a long and beautiful night of sleep alongside the man she loved more than life itself.

"It's a good life," she whispered in the mirror. "And it's probably more than I deserve, but I'll take it anyhow."

Chapter Thirteen

Cecily Monahan was a retired school teacher and now a full-time seamstress hired to stitch up everything from newborn outfits to wedding gowns to curtains and sails for sailboats. Since her retirement from the same high school where Cora had worked as both a theater director and English teacher, Cecily offered her services to the community theater troupe, throwing herself into creating all costumes for every character.

It was Monday, February twenty-second, and Cecily and her eldest daughter had just arrived backstage with several costumes wrapped up in protective plastic. They bustled to the clothing stand and latched each of the hangers upon the iron with Cecily muttering how best to organize them. When Lola released them from the final minutes of their rigorous rehearsal, the actors within the musical itself scattered off the stage to find them. Several of the little girls who'd played in other productions squealed excitedly at Cecily's arrival. Costumes were far more fun than wearing your everyday garb on stage.

Costumes meant that your character was finally coming to life.

Cecily greeted Cora warmly with a delicate kiss on the cheek, something she'd picked up when she'd taken a costume designing course in Paris during the summer after her retirement. Cora wasn't sure if she resented the kiss more or the fact that Cecily had spent all that time alone in Paris. Unlike Cora, Cecily had divorced her husband years ago and decided to live out a life of single-dom, creeping through her fifties and now early sixties without a care in the world. How wretched for Cora that she'd actually wanted a happily ever after with Victor. If only she could be like Cecily— alive, confident, and free from sorrow.

"Such a sad thing to walk through those doors and know Victor's not here," Cecily said to Cora as Cora settled into the chair alongside the clothing rack.

Cora made a soft, strange sound in her throat. It sounded like an animal. When she lifted her eyes, she was surprised to find Hank, Daddy Warbucks, stationed a little bit away. He had his hands in his pockets, and his eyes were soulful, connecting with hers. Had he heard what Cecily had said to her? Was this an offering of pity? Did Cora even want to accept that?

"But I really did go all-out on your costumes, you beautiful thing," Cecily told Cora as she pulled out several items of clothing. "Miss Hannigan has some of the best clothing of the entire production. Of course, I did have a blast making a little red dress for Miss Annie." Cecily turned to find Jenny, the lead, seated on a high stool eating a granola bar and humming to herself nervously. "It must be stressful, being so young with so much responsibility. But anyway, darling." Cecily's eyes returned to Cora's in preparation to deliver more soul-crushing words about Victor.

"Hello." Hank stepped forward to greet Cecily, interrupting her.

"Oh, hello." Cecily's eyes widened with surprise. "You must be new!"

"I am." Hank slid a hand across the thick, luscious hair at the top of his head. "I was a teenager on the island, but I moved off when I was eighteen or nineteen. I've just returned and thought to myself, community theater? Back in New Jersey, I hadn't done it for years, but here I am, back at it again."

"How long did you take off since your last performance?" Cora was genuinely shocked. The fact that he'd taken on a role as big as Daddy Warbucks after not using his acting chops for so long was mesmerizing to her.

Hank shrugged. "I was quite busy for a few decades—my children, my job, chores, and all the things that add up in life. And now, it's just me. My ex-wife always said I had a flair for the dramatic."

Cecily laughed good-naturedly and then flashed Cora a knowing smile. What was this smile meant to convey? Did Cecily like Hank? Was she on the verge of flirtation? Was Hank flirting with Cecily?

"I think my ex-husband said the same thing about me," Cecily told him. "But I prefer to keep my work backstage."

"And such fine work it is," Hank complimented, watching as Cora removed her first outfit from the hanger.

Cecily blushed like a teenage girl. Cora wanted to scold her, but she wasn't entirely sure where this instinct came from. She genuinely liked Cecily, or always had before.

"I'll just give this a try," Cora told her.

"Just like every other time before," Cecily sing-songed. "And Hank? I have the perfect Daddy Warbucks outfit for you."

Cora stepped into the small dressing room area where three little girls from the musical's orphanage sputtered around, giggling in their garments. Cora stood in the corner and changed timidly, feeling like an old maid compared to these confident little girls with their soft cheeks and long luscious hair. When Cora left the dressing room, she found Hank already in his Daddy Warbucks tuxedo as Cecily circled him, ensuring the fit was appropriate.

"There you are."

Cora spun on her heel to find Lola Sheridan, her large folder of notes and scripts pressed against her chest and her eyes catching the soft lights of backstage.

"You look fantastic," Lola told her, eyeing her Miss Hannigan outfit. "I couldn't have imagined it better."

"Cecily's the best," Cora replied in a tone that didn't convince her at all.

"She must be." Lola eyed Cecily and Hank once more, then leaned against the nearest wall as her knees smacked together beneath her. "Pardon me, Cora. I'm so exhausted and overwhelmed by the week ahead. I have three performances, a little birthday party for my grand-son, and the wedding to the love of my life."

"That makes my head spin," Cora breathed.

"Come on. You? You're just about as cool as a cucum-ber," Lola teased.

"I don't know about that."

Lola shrugged and lifted herself back up slowly so that her neck creaked. "I'm not sure I could ever thank you enough for all the help you've given me over the past six weeks. It's been such a prosperous time with you as the unofficial director of this musical."

"Nonsense," Cora told her. "You've been the director."

"And you've been my guiding light," Lola said.

Cora smiled inwardly and then glanced nervously back toward Hank. On cue, Cecily bustled toward her, her voice overly bright as she began to assess Cora's wardrobe and any additional fixes that needed to be done prior to Wednesday's dress rehearsal. Jenny jumped toward Lola to ask her about one of the musical numbers later in the show while Hank again disappeared through the dark shadows backstage.

After Cora had finalized each of her stage outfits for the show, she dressed once more in her jeans and her black turtleneck and shoved her feet into her size six tennis shoes. Victor had always teased her about her tiny ballerina feet. As she grew older, Cora worried they wouldn't be strong enough to keep her going. The bones creaked oddly beneath her sometimes; it felt like a threat.

"See you tomorrow, everyone!" Lola called from where she sat alongside Audrey and Amanda. Audrey ate a large chocolate chip cookie while Amanda scribbled additional notes. "And remember to be costume ready on Wednesday! Dress rehearsal means we do everything exactly like opening night. It's a big deal, people."

Cora gathered her things and headed toward the hallway behind the auditorium, where the door opened toward the parking lot and the downtown street she normally took to walk home. Just before she pressed open the glass door to retreat, she heard her name.

"Cora!"

She froze. A creeping sensation rose up her spine and along her shoulders and neck. When she turned around to find Hank all but running toward her, she couldn't help but give him a confused smile. He ran toward her like a teenager, joyful and excited about the life he still had to live.

"Hi, there." She couldn't help but feel a smidgeon of his happiness. There was something about the rush leading up to the first performance. The people who'd worked hard alongside you were more than friends. Their passions aligned with yours; their hearts beat in time to the same song.

"I thought I'd never get away from that Cecily woman," Hank stated as they stepped through the door.

Cora let out a surprised laugh. Her tennis shoes slipped slightly across the icy sidewalk, and in the strange moment that followed, Hank grabbed her elbow to steady her. The feel of his touch, even through her thick winter coat, made her heart jump into her throat. She'd experienced touch in various ways— through other actors in the musical and through the annoying kiss of Cecily, the costume manager. But this felt different. This was meant for Cora and Cora alone— not Miss Hannigan.

"Gosh, thank you. I don't know what got into me," she said.

"Nothing got into you. They just haven't taken care of this sidewalk very well this winter," Hank returned.

"We've had a lot of very cold days," Cora pointed out. "I'm sure it's difficult to keep up with."

Hank's smile was crooked. Perhaps some might have called it handsome.

"Are you always so empathetic?" Hank asked her.

"I don't suppose empathy's such a bad thing."

"No. I think it might be the most important thing there is," Hank said.

"Especially if you're an actor," Cora stated.

"As I said, I'm pretty new at this."

"It's difficult to believe," Cora told him. "You and Lola are both newbies, yet both of you are arguably fantastic at what you've chosen to do."

"Don't compliment me so soon before the show," Hank warned her playfully. "I might get bigheaded and mess up my lines."

"Good point," Cora noted. "Silly of me not to think of theater rhetoric."

Hank laughed as they continued to walk along the sidewalk, headed straight into town. Cora wondered if he lived near her place.

"You mentioned that you were a teenager on the island?" Cora asked.

"That's right," he said. He then lowered his voice to add, "I went to school with Lola's mother, Anna, and her sister, Willa. I was closer in age to Willa, but Willa left when we were kids. I imagine she doesn't remember me."

Cora's heartbeat quickened. "Goodness. You knew Anna Sheridan before she..."

"Before she was Anna Sheridan. Yep," Hank affirmed. "She had quite a violent family. You could always hear one of the parents screaming when you walked past her place. Nobody was surprised when she hooked up with Wes so quickly after graduation. She had to get out of that house."

Cora nodded, sorrowful for a long-ago past that still cast its shadow over the present.

"It's pretty wild to me just how similar Lola is to Anna," Hank continued. "From what I remember, they have similar mannerisms. They say the same sorts of things and wear their hair the same."

Cora blinked back tears. She hated when anyone wept for her personal sorrows, as they didn't belong to them.

"I believe Anna died when Lola was eleven," Cora breathed. "I suppose that means she never really knew her."

"Such a tragedy." Hank shook his head as he continued alongside Cora.

The streetlight sparkled across the newly fallen snow. Cora lifted her eyes toward the impenetrable black sky, which reflected no stars. Sometimes it was very apparent to her that they lived on a rock floating in the center of the Atlantic.

"You've already taught me a great deal about the theater, Cora," Hank told her softly as they neared her door. "I've watched your mannerisms, the way you hold yourself on stage, and the way you say your lines. You're a real professional. And one afternoon, you mentioned an acting book you read when you were just starting out. I immediately purchased it and read it all the way through on a random Sunday in January. It made me think about acting so differently. It gave me a real voice."

They'd suddenly arrived before Cora's house. Her heart quickened at the beautiful glow of his eyes, which seemed to take in the vision of her. It was as though he never needed to see another woman.

Invite him in for tea, she told herself.

But imaginary stones thudded in her stomach. She shook her head against the strange thoughts that simmered in the back of her mind. She couldn't. No man had entered her house since Victor's death.

"This is me," she told him firmly. "Thank you for walking me home. And thank you for saying that about the acting. It means a lot to me to work alongside other actors who uphold the art the way you seem to."

Hank bowed his head gently, maintaining eye contact. "It's my pleasure. Have a beautiful night, Cora. I'll see you tomorrow."

Chapter Fourteen

Wednesday's dress rehearsal couldn't have been a bigger disaster. Lola, Audrey, and Amanda watched with captivated eyes from their audience seats as everyone from Daddy Warbucks to Annie skipped over lines, stumbled on musical numbers, and generally walked around like lost puppies on stage. Naturally, Cora's Miss Hannigan was a perpetual knock-out, essentially saving the dress rehearsal from out-and-out failure.

After the thick red curtain closed, Lola stood, her frustration brimming, and called the cast members back out onto the stage. One after another, they returned, still in costume, and listened as Lola told them, in no uncertain circumstances, that they were better than the performance they'd just put on, and they knew it. It was a kind of speech Lola hadn't thought herself capable of— a speech that thrilled Lola to say, as she felt herself generating pride and assurance within the rest of the musical team members.

"Amanda? Audrey? Do you have anything to say

before we depart for the night?" Lola asked her assistant directors.

Audrey burst to her feet and clapped her hands wildly. "You've rehearsed yourselves silly. You've memorized line after line, dance number after dance number. Now, it's up to you to show off all you've done to the rest of Martha's Vineyard. I've spent the past several weeks bragging about your musicality and your passion. Don't disappoint me!" Audrey's eyes widened as she turned to nod toward Amanda. "Take it away, Amanda."

Amanda blushed and stood to greet them timidly. "I think my aunt Lola and cousin Audrey have both said everything that needs to be said. Just know that I believe in you. And we've been through this great journey together, one that I'll never forget."

Back in the car, Audrey and Amanda both teased one another about the cheesiness of their dress rehearsal speeches.

"We've been on this great journey together," Audrey said in a sing-song voice as Amanda stuck out her tongue playfully.

"We had to say the right things after that dress rehearsal. We couldn't let them stew in disappointment," Amanda pointed out. "Gosh, it was such a mess from the get-go."

"They've never performed so badly," Lola agreed from the driver's seat. "I should have called it off halfway through and made them restart."

"Maybe this means they got it out of their system," Audrey tried.

"There's no way it will be that bad tomorrow," Amanda agreed. "If it is, then we should all retire from the theater for good."

Lola parked in the driveway outside Susan's gorgeous house, alongside Scott's truck, Sam's car, and Noah's Jeep.

"We've got a full house for dinner tonight," Lola teased.

"Is Tommy coming tonight?" Audrey asked.

"No. He told Scott he'd sleep in Boston tonight and then head back to the island in the morning on a freight," Lola explained.

"He's working so hard," Amanda said.

"I've missed him," Lola admitted as she turned the engine off and looked at her niece. "But I've been so busy with the musical. I imagine next week we'll spend a whole lot of time hanging around the house, eating snacks, and going on long walks through the woods hunting for Dad's favorite birds."

"And making out," Audrey countered.

"Oh my gosh, Audrey." Amanda rolled her eyes as her smile crept from ear to ear. "You perv."

Inside, they found Sam, Noah, Grandpa Wes, and Kellan amid a passionate and incredibly competitive game of euchre, a card game that required them to team up. Grandpa Wes and Kellan had become a powerful team with many within the Sheridan clan suggesting they could read one another's minds. It was a remarkable thing for Lola, watching her father battle dementia and also play a whip-smart card game. He still contained multitudes. It was a marvel.

"Hey! It's our thespians!" Noah leaped up to kiss Audrey on the lips without a care in the world that her grandfather sat mere feet away. Audrey bent back romantically so that her hair fell down her back.

"How was dress rehearsal?" Sam, who worked for the

family, was a bit less overt about his feelings for Amanda. He stood and hugged her gently, only his eyes giving his immense love away.

"A disaster," Lola explained.

"Uh-oh." Noah laughed outright. "What does that mean for tomorrow?"

"It means we're going to be crossing our fingers and toes for luck," Audrey joked.

"And praying that little Annie hits all those high notes," Amanda added, her eyes widening.

"We just made some hot chocolate," Grandpa Wes told the girls. "I reckon that'll fix your night."

Christine appeared at the base of the staircase with little Mia cocooned against her chest. "Max just fell asleep upstairs, Aud," she explained in greeting.

"Oh gosh, thank you," Audrey replied.

"He's a little dreamboat," Christine said. "Almost one year old now!"

"Hard to believe that was all nearly a year ago." Audrey lifted her eyes toward Noah, whom she'd met outside the NICU as Max had struggled for his life. "I couldn't be more grateful for all that's happened."

Sam headed for the kitchen to brew up another round of hot chocolate for the new arrivals. Lola collapsed in the chair alongside her father as Kellan returned the playing cards to their packaging. Lola placed her head on her father's shoulder as the kettle bubbled hot water in the kitchen.

"Just a few more days now, Little Lola," her father said in a raspy voice, placing his hand gently on the top of her head and stroking the softness of her hair. "I still remember how I felt during the days before I married your mother."

"What did you feel like?" Lola's throat tightened with the sorrow that she'd struggled to ignore. She'd now lived two years longer than her mother, who'd died at thirty-eight. What's more— she ached with a strange sensation that she wanted to discuss the intricacies of falling in love and commitment with someone like her mother. She supposed she could try Aunt Willa out for that conversation, especially as she'd become a sort of stand-in mother in recent weeks. Even still, there would be no one on the planet like Anna Sheridan ever again.

"I felt like my life was about to begin with a whole new set of rules and a whole new list of things to be grateful for," Grandpa Wes breathed. "But I realized I had my foot on the gas pedal, and there wasn't a brake. Life was full speed ahead after that: babies and house bills and duties with the Sunrise Cove. I was grateful, so grateful to fall asleep in bed with your mother every night. But I wish I could take back that moment right before it all began. I wish I could feel what you're feeling right now. This feeling of 'before.' This feeling that it's all about to begin."

Lola's eyes filled with tears. Her father had built a sort of poetry around the nature of his earlier life. As she struggled to think of how to respond, there was the *whack-whack-whack* of footfalls in the mudroom. A split second later, Susan appeared, her hair damp from a new snowfall. Her eyes widened as she pulled off her coat.

"Mom! What's up?" Amanda looked at her mother curiously, reaching for her coat.

"It's really coming down out there," Susan explained.

As Amanda disappeared to hang Susan's coat, Susan grabbed the remote control and flicked on the television, which ordinarily remained off when so many of the

Sheridan family congregated together. Susan often complained of the "white noise" of the television and how much she detested it. Now, she flicked toward the weather channel, where a bright banner was positioned at the bottom.

WINTER STORM WARNING FOR WEDNESDAY NIGHT AND THURSDAY MORNING.

"Uh-oh." Audrey popped out of Noah's arms and jumped onto the couch to lean toward the television.

The meteorologist explained that a winter storm was headed directly toward Martha's Vineyard, bringing with it approximately eight inches of snow. Lola's heart thudded with fear. She headed for the back window, where she turned on the light and caught the reflection of the snowflakes outside. They were thick, fluffy, and definitely going to stick to the ground for good.

Lola's phone buzzed in her pocket.

TOMMY: Looks like a storm is headed right for us.

TOMMY: I hope I can get back on the island.

TOMMY: If not, I'll meet you at the altar. I'll be the one in the freight boat uniform.

LOLA: That's when you look the most handsome, anyway.

LOLA: I love you. Be safe out there.

Christine appeared alongside Lola and peered out the window. Her hand was wrapped gently around little sleeping Mia's head.

"If the storm's only for tonight and tomorrow, I don't think you should worry yourself about the wedding," Christine told Lola as though she could read her mind.

"It'll be fine," Lola affirmed. "I have to be a force of positivity right now. Even if I don't believe in it."

"Why don't you sit down and drink your hot cocoa, Lola?" her father asked gently. "I'm sure Kellan and I could be convinced to destroy you and another partner at euchre."

Lola laughed outright, circled back, and dropped into a dining room chair. Kellan quickly removed the cards and shuffled as Lola hand-selected Noah to be her new euchre partner. If this was her daughter's chosen love, Lola wanted to get to know him better, to dig into his personality and know what sorts of things made him laugh. It was a remarkable thing to watch her daughter fall in love. It belonged on the long list of other things she'd watched Audrey do over the years, like take her first step, speak her first word, write her first article, and have her first child.

After several rounds of euchre, bouts of ridiculous laughter, and a silly episode of *The Office* on television, Susan announced that the driveway and roads were too snowy for Lola to return to her cabin and Christine to return to her home with Zach.

"We need you to stay the night," Susan said firmly. "If the roads are cleared tomorrow, you can find your way back."

"Okay, Miss Bossy," Lola teased.

"Aye aye, Captain," Christine returned.

On cue, Max let out a loud squeal which spit out of the baby monitor on the counter. Audrey hustled upstairs to wrap him up in winter garb and carry him back to the

Sheridan House, where she, Amanda, and Grandpa Wes resided. Christine decided to stay in Susan's guest room while Lola walked through the winter wonderland back toward the Sheridan House with Grandpa Wes, Audrey, and Amanda. It was a funny thing watching Audrey, Amanda, and Grandpa Wes all together. The three of them had created quite a rapport, with Audrey teasing the living daylights out of her grandfather and Amanda acting as the mirror image of her mother, reeling both of them in. Lola had never had such a powerful relationship with Wes, and she felt oddly left out of what the three of them had, even as she was grateful for it.

Max fell back asleep almost as soon as he was back in his crib upstairs in Audrey's bedroom, which had once been Lola's back in her teenage years. Lola and Audrey sat on the top step of the creaky house as the wind roared outside. Downstairs, Wes's door clicked closed about a minute before Amanda's.

"Do you still like living in this house?" Lola breathed.

Audrey nodded. "I love it. Amanda and Grandpa Wes are the best roommates I've ever had. Especially after last semester at Penn State, it feels like a dream come true."

Lola dipped her head against the wall and eyed her beautiful daughter. It was often like looking at an old photograph of herself.

"Do you think you and Noah are headed toward something?" Lola asked her softly. She wasn't entirely sure why she wanted to know the answer.

The window in the nearest bedroom caught the light of the moon. It drew a sharp white across Audrey's beautiful face as she considered the question.

"To be honest, Mom. I'm only twenty years old, and

although I've had to grow up ridiculously fast in many different ways, I'm still trying to enjoy the little moments, even if they aren't forever. I'm enjoying the way Noah makes me laugh until I cry, and the way he teases Grandpa Wes about his card playing, and the way Max giggles when Noah lifts him. There are so many beautiful things to witness." She then shrugged and added, "Maybe when I'm twenty-one in April, I'll think about what it means to grow up and make big life-altering decisions."

Lola laughed and closed her eyes as exhaustion simmered through her. "I'm four days away from one of the biggest decisions I've ever made. I never thought I'd take this step. I always spoke just the way you're speaking — about acknowledging the beauty of the here and now and not needing the finality of everything else."

Audrey grabbed her mother's hand. Lola's eyes opened once more in surprise.

"What you're doing is more than acknowledging the beauty of the here and now," Audrey told her firmly. "You're acknowledging the beauty of what you and Tommy have built and will continue to build together. At twenty, I don't know if I have the strength to build something like that. But you do, Mom. You do, and you deserve all of it."

Chapter Fifteen

A soft and shimmering white light flickered through the curtains in the upstairs bedroom. Lola's eyes parted to the heavenly sight as she struggled for a moment to remember precisely where she woke. Slowly, the upstairs bedroom of the Sheridan House came into focus. A moment later, as though he recognized that Lola needed some kind of soundtrack, Max's early morning squeal erupted through the top floor before it fell back into one of his confident, silly giggles.

Lola lifted herself, curled herself into a ball, and brought the curtain to the side to peer out. Just as the meteorologist had predicted, the late February night had greeted them with what seemed to be eight inches of snow. It toiled over the rooftop of the Sheridan House and bent the surrounding tree limbs toward the ground. Eastward, the sun lifted its head from the treetops, confident and sure after a night of clouds and storms. It was six forty-five in the morning, but Lola already felt sure that there wouldn't be a whole lot of moving around on the island. Not until the snow was cleared, anyway.

This meant that the opening night of *Annie* was no longer a sure thing.

Lola fell back into the clean white sheets of the upstairs bed and grabbed her phone from the bedside table. To her delight, several messages from Tommy awaited her, spanning from three thirty in the morning to just before six.

> TOMMY: Eight inches over here. Scott says no freight this morning, so I'm going to head back to bed. Love you.

> TOMMY: Can't sleep. I feel so excited to get back on the island and make you my wife.

> TOMMY: I wish you were here beside me. I hate these lonely nights and mornings.

> TOMMY: Love you, Lola.

Lola curled into a tighter ball and closed her eyes. In the next room, Audrey cooed with Max, opening his day with optimism and unfiltered joy. Lola remembered those early mornings with Audrey when she'd looked up at Lola from the depths of her crib and made Lola believe in the beauty of motherhood, of the unique connection between a mother and her baby. For years, Lola hadn't fully understood where she ended and her baby began. And then, all at once, her baby had her own baby, and Lola lay in the next-door room alone.

When Lola recognized that she wouldn't be able to fall back asleep, she donned her robe and made her way downstairs to find Grandpa Wes and Amanda seated at the breakfast table, both with steaming mugs of coffee and crossword puzzles before them. The toast popped up from the toaster as Amanda greeted her warmly.

"Want something to eat?"

"I'm okay for now."

Lola grinned sleepily and reached for the pot of coffee. When she sat at the table alongside her niece and father, the light off the snow nearly blinded her. It was a severe white, almost sinister in its beauty. Wes took a large bite of toast and crunched joyously as he continued to piece through his crossword. This was the definition of coziness, Lola knew. When her daughter and Max appeared downstairs, both hungry and eager for the day ahead, Lola felt the final pieces of the puzzle click into place. Perhaps this was what she needed, especially so soon before her big day.

"Look!" Audrey called from the back window. "Kellan and Noah are shoveling the driveway!"

"You're kidding," Lola replied as she shuffled toward the back to watch. "How did Noah get over here so early this morning?"

"His snowmobile is parked over there," Audrey pointed toward the line of trees. "My knight in shining armor!"

"It's not like he can shovel us all the way to town," Amanda pointed out. "We're more or less stuck here for the day."

"They'll plow us out by the afternoon," Grandpa Wes said, speaking with authority after seventy years on the island. "Meanwhile, I suggest that we get dressed up to go appreciate the beautiful winter wonderland that God gave us this morning. Who's with me?"

Just past eight thirty in the morning, Lola, Audrey, Amanda, Max, and Grandpa Wes donned several layers, mittens and hats, scarves and boots, and headed out into the shimmering white of the morning. Grandpa Wes's binoculars banged away on his chest as he stepped toward Kellan to greet him warmly.

"Look at you. Hard at work!" he hollered to his step-grandson.

Amanda carried Max outside as Audrey rushed through the snow to greet Noah with a sloppy kiss.

"When did you get so nice?" Audrey asked Noah, teasing him.

"What are you talking about? I've always been nice," Noah replied tenderly just before he placed another kiss on her lips.

"Hey! Who's out there so early in the morning?" This was Susan's voice, crying out from her driveway on the other side of the line of trees.

"Come over here!" Lola called back. "I know for a fact you've got the skills we need to make a perfect snowman."

Susan cackled like a much younger version of herself. After a few moments more, there came the sound of her feet crushing through the snow. She appeared, rotund in her winter gear, a smile electric on her bright red face.

"What are you waiting for?" Susan called. "Let's roll that snowman."

"Where's Christine?" Amanda asked.

"Did someone say my name?" Christine appeared through the trees a second later with little Mia wrapped as snug as a bug in a rug within her winter clothing.

"You were never one for winter festivities, Christine," Susan pointed out as she bent low to begin rolling the snowman's torso.

"I don't know what you're talking about," Christine returned.

"Yeah. Miss Teenage Angst didn't have time to make snowmen with me back in the old days," Lola teased.

"You know I needed time to process my feelings in my bedroom alone," Christine joked. "Hours and hours of time to listen to my tapes and write in my journal."

Suddenly, there came a *whack*. Kellan howled, "What was that for?" as he whipped around to glare at Grandpa Wes. Grandpa Wes laughed outright and bent down to make another snowball, which he tossed immediately at Kellan.

"Now you asked for it, old man!" Kellan called as he dropped his shovel and formed a snowball to throw back. It exploded on Grandpa Wes's chest, casting white fluff in all directions.

"Oh goodness..." Christine bucked back from the line of fire to protect Mia. Amanda joined her with Max flailing around excitedly in her arms.

Audrey, Noah, Lola, Grandpa Wes, Kellan, and Susan began to whip snowballs at one another, hiding behind trees and vehicles and howling with laughter. After ten to fifteen minutes, Grandpa Wes cried, "Wait! Wait just a gosh-darn second!"

The warring Sheridan clan stopped, some with snowballs lifted midair. Grandpa Wes raised a finger and pointed toward the farther treetops, where, sure enough, that bright-red cardinal (perhaps even the same one) was poised up high. The cardinal seemed to peer down at them, watching their winter slaughter.

"It's beautiful," Christine breathed from the back porch.

The cardinal watched them for what seemed to be a

full minute before he flew skyward once more, careening across the severe blue of the sky. After that, they tore through the snow once more, flailing snowballs and building a six-foot-tall snowman (the tallest they'd ever seen). Eventually, the frigid air led them to stomp their boots off in the mudroom before midmorning coffee and biscuits, where Lola, Amanda, and Audrey reassessed the plan for the day ahead.

"School was canceled. The roads won't be cleared till late afternoon," Amanda reported. "And I don't think we can expect anyone at the auditorium for opening night."

Lola puffed out her cheeks. "I hate to disappoint the crew. We've all worked so hard for this."

"But you'll have Friday and Saturday night," Grandpa Wes pointed out. "Plenty of time for everyone on the island to see what you've done."

"I'll check the weather and make sure no more snow is headed our way," Amanda said as she grabbed her phone to investigate her weather app. "Tomorrow, Saturday, and Sunday are crystal clear. The musical's on— as is the wedding."

"And the birthday party Saturday afternoon!" Audrey cried as she twirled in a circle with Max in her arms. He squealed appreciatively as though he knew it was nearly his first birthday.

Meanwhile, Lola scribed an email to the cast and crew of *Annie*.

Dear Cast and Crew,

Happy Snow Day!

This morning, I awoke to a winter wonderland— proof of the rather sad truth that we'll have to push back our opening night to tomorrow.

I hope you're all having cozy mornings with your nearest and dearest.

She then stopped and reread what she'd written, remembering those in the cast who lived alone and had no one like Cora. She hurriedly deleted the last line and continued on.

It was clear to me that we suffered from stage jitters last night at dress rehearsal, which is only natural. That said, tomorrow, I'd like to meet at the auditorium extra early, around three fifteen, to go over a few of the parts we stumbled over, get a good warm-up for our voices, and shake the jitters out.

So enjoy the day ahead. Relax. Unwind. And focus on tomorrow's opening night. After the hard work you've put in, you deserve nothing but fame and glory. Let's show Martha's Vineyard what we've got!

Love, Lola

Lola reread the email aloud for Amanda and Audrey, who approved. Immediately after she sent it, Lola received a call from Charlotte, whom she put on speakerphone.

"Hi, Charlotte! I'm here with just about everyone who matters," Lola said.

"Hi, everyone who matters!" Charlotte echoed. "This is some snow, isn't it? But I've already checked the weather. We're in the clear for the weekend ahead. The wedding is a go!"

"We did, too. How did it go with those last RSVPs?"

"Everyone RSVP'd yes," Charlotte reported. "The caterer's ready. The cake's perfect. Claire's obsessively finalizing your flower arrangements. What else? Gosh, I had this long list of to-dos, and it's miraculously finished. What am I going to do with myself now?"

"Relax? Enjoy yourself? Something like that?" Lola told her.

"Yeah, right. Everett and Rachel will tell you that I only enjoy myself if I have a project to do," Charlotte joked.

"It's true!" This was Rachel, hollering out on the other end of the line.

"I just hope the groom will be able to get back on the island. He couldn't get to the freight this morning."

"Goodness," Charlotte said. "Well, if he can't make it, we'll arrange for a stand-in groom."

"Fantastic. You know the only important part of this is that I get married. I don't really care who the groom is," Lola jested, bubbling with laughter.

"Oh, I know."

The wintery afternoon continued after that, with the Sheridan clan jumping from the Sheridan House to Susan's place next door for warm beef stew, hot chocolate and tea, snacks, games of cards, more snowball fights, and plenty of sky-watching for some of Wes's favorite birds. By four o'clock, the lot of them were exhausted, with Grandpa Wes, Christine, Mia, and Noah all collapsing on Susan's couch for accidental and spontaneous naps.

Later on, Lola, Christine, and Susan sat alone around the Sheridan House table as the others collected in various locations across the two houses, either playing games, watching television, or preparing for another trek through the snow. The three original Sheridan Sisters remained silent, each heavy with their own thoughts. And all the while, an old photograph of Anna Sheridan stood on high, watching over them— a constant reminder of their connection to the past, even as they marched bravely toward the future.

Chapter Sixteen

The following afternoon at three fifteen sharp, Lola stood center stage at the downtown auditorium. She peered down at the cast and crew for Martha's Vineyard performance of *Annie*, set to begin at seven thirty that evening. Lola wore a simple black turtleneck, a pair of dark jeans, and a pair of black tennis shoes with very little makeup. She'd once seen a documentary about a female film director who, when interviewed, had dressed simply, describing her fashion as "behind the scenes to allow whatever story she worked on flourish outside of her."

"Today's the big day," Lola told her cast and crew. "I want each and every one of you to turn off your phones and really focus here. This stage is now your world. *Annie* is now the only story you know. Your character is you. And if you're backstage crew— lighting or otherwise— you're like the sun and the moon and the stars for the cast. You're like oxygen. Nobody else can exist without you."

Lola watched as the cast and crew grabbed their cell phones and set them to OFF. There was finality in the way they moved from the auditorium seats to backstage. Soon, they would warm up their voices, stretch their arms and legs, and head straight to their first position for the opening moments of the musical. Annie, played by Jenny, seemed especially laser-focused. When Lola's eyes met hers, Jenny gave her only a firm nod in greeting, as though speaking anything out of character was a no-go for her.

Over the next three hours, Lola's team hit the parts of the musical that they'd stumbled over on Wednesday. They ran and re-ran lines. They hit their marks, missed their marks, and then hit them again. The orchestra pit, a marvelous ensemble of local musicians, played the same bars of the same songs over and over again to allow the actors to fine-tune what they'd learned.

By the time six thirty came around, Lola, Audrey, and Amanda exchanged stoic glances. It was time that they cut the rehearsals and send the crew backstage to get ready for the main show. Very soon, the ticket booth workers would arrive. Tables would be set up in the back hallways to sell refreshments like popcorn, pretzels, and large sodas. Parents would arrive extra early to get good seats so they could take perfect photos of their children on stage. The Sheridan clan alone would probably take up at least twelve to fifteen seats near the front, eliminating others' chances of really stellar views. With Rachel, Gail, and Abby as orphans and Audrey, Amanda, and Lola as directors, they had a real right to see the production up close.

"That went really well, I think," Amanda said as she went over her notes from the previous three hours of rehearsal. "I was surprised when Jenny hit that note perfectly."

"I'm not," Lola returned. "I have a feeling she spent

all day yesterday with her mom at the piano, belting out song after song until she got it right."

"Meanwhile, all we did yesterday was play in the snow," Audrey joked. "Poor girl. So much weight on her shoulders!"

"But she's going to knock it out of the park," Lola affirmed. "Gosh, I'm just so proud of everyone. It was a quick seven weeks, but we learned all we could over that time. I don't know about you, but I feel like a different woman at the end of that seven weeks than I was at the beginning. It almost felt like working on this big production with this beautiful group of individuals taught me something about myself."

Amanda and Audrey nodded.

"It makes me want to continue to be involved in something like this," Audrey confessed. "To get to know these people and allow us to dig deeper into the Martha's Vineyard community."

"Maybe Max will play Oliver Twist on stage in a few years," Amanda teased.

Audrey's eyes watered with excitement. "He'll be a star!"

"Uh-oh. Stage Mom alert..." Amanda said with a roll of her eyes.

As the cousins teased one another, swapping gossip and discussing their boyfriends, Lola grabbed her phone to text Tommy. Apparently, he hadn't been able to leave the mainland that morning, either, but planned to return the following morning. "I'll be in time for Max's birthday, the last night of the musical, and of course, Sunday's big day."

But when Lola turned her phone back on, she received a smattering of missed call notifications and text messages from her father, Susan, Christine, Lola, Zach, and Tommy.

> SUSAN: Check the weather! The storm has shifted! Headed straight for the island!

> CHRISTINE: Have you looked outside? It's coming down fast...

> ZACH: Hey! Christine says this might be the last chance if you need someone to pick you up.

> SCOTT: Missed call.

> DAD: Hey, honey! Are you safe out there? Did you start rehearsal already?

> TOMMY: Missed call.

> TOMMY: Missed call.

> TOMMY: Babe, answer your phone.

Lola's heart rammed against her rib cage. Abruptly, she rushed down the aisle and headed for the back hallway. Once there, a large floor-to-ceiling glass door opened out onto the parking lot. As it was past six thirty and already black with night, Lola couldn't see far beyond the window. She could, however, see that in the previous three and a half hours, perhaps two feet of snow had been dumped on the snow that already remained outside. As she stared, thick globs of white snowflakes continued to fall from the sky with no indication of letting up.

"Oh my gosh..." Lola breathed. She hustled for the door

and blinked further out at the parking lot, where every single vehicle was buried deep within the white. She pressed a hand on the glass and exhaled all the air from her lungs. How had this happened? How had the storm shifted?

Lola turned back and walked down the hallway with her chin pointed toward the ground. The hallway seemed especially empty, as it was supposed to already be echoing with conversation from the parents who'd volunteered to set up ticket selling areas and drink and snack tables. Naturally, those parents hadn't been able to drive to the auditorium to begin the setup. Everyone was latched away in their cozy houses across the island.

And Lola, Audrey, Amanda, and the rest of the cast and crew of *Annie* were stranded at the downtown auditorium, preparing for a show that wouldn't go on.

When Lola returned to the auditorium, she found Amanda and Audrey still in an excited conversation about Noah and Sam.

"But he has this adorable habit where he snores once and then wakes himself up," Amanda said. "He doesn't know about it. It's like my private joke."

Audrey howled with laughter, pressing her hand against her stomach. However, when she lifted her eyes toward Lola's, all the color drained from her cheeks. "Mom? What's wrong? You look—"

Lola's face was marred with panic. She pressed a hand across her forehead as the shock of the snow took hold of her.

"Aunt Lola? What's wrong?" Amanda asked, her voice rasping.

"I just... I just looked outside..." Lola shook her head. "And there's at least two feet more of snow outside. It came down so quickly. Nobody saw it coming. I'm sure everyone's stranded in their homes."

"What?" Audrey shrieked and rushed for the back hallway with Amanda hot on her heels. In a few minutes, they returned wearing their own sad-sack expressions. Audrey ran her fingers through her hair, exasperated. "I've never seen a blizzard like that."

Amanda grabbed her phone to turn it on. After the screen lit up again, she announced, "Yep. Service is already down."

"What?" Audrey cried, checking her phone immediately after. "Oh gosh. Mom." Audrey's eyes widened. "Mom, I'm so sorry."

"I have to go tell everyone backstage," Lola said. "I think everyone left their phones out here. They won't know yet."

Lola marched somberly backstage, with Amanda and Audrey trailing her. As they walked, the roar of the cast and crew grew louder, more frenetic. The energy was like a circus. Little girls jumped around joyously, already wearing their little dresses for the orphanage scenes. Daddy Warbucks marched past, wearing his bald cap. Miss Hannigan grinned excitedly as Cecily, the costume director, perfected her makeup. Cora hadn't looked so joyous in ages— a fact that twisted Lola's gut. This was to be her debut after her husband's death. This was to be her fresh start.

But it wasn't going to happen.

"Everyone, please, can I have your attention," Lola began from the center of the shadowy backstage area. "I have an announcement. And I'm sorry to say, but it's not good news."

Chapter Seventeen

F ollowing Lola's announcement, *Annie's* cast and crew members fell into an immediate state of duress. The littler orphans wrapped their arms around the older ones and shook with tears. However, Rachel, Gail, and Abby seemed to take the news in stride, whispering to one another about the probability of an overnight sleepover at the auditorium. Miss Hannigan's brother, "Rooster," played by a man in his early forties, gossiped with the woman who played Grace Farrell, saying, "I reckon there's some food in the cafeteria down the hall. They always have big celebrations here— birthdays and retirement parties and graduations. I'm sure they're well-stocked. We won't starve."

Cora, for her part, felt just about as low as ever. She remained in her Miss Hannigan costume with a full face of makeup, feeling foolish. Cecily chattered beside her, her brow furrowed with worry. Cora couldn't make out what she said. Midway through Cecily's chatter, Cora stepped off to the side and fled for one of the back hallways, where she could stand in the silence of herself and feel all that she needed to feel.

Once in the back hallway, Cora leaned heavily against the wide white wall, closed her eyes, and allowed the first of probably many tears to fall. When opening night had been canceled the day before, she had stayed in her robe all morning and afternoon, playing Miss Hannigan tunes on her piano and perfecting her voice for the upcoming performance. She'd felt Victor there alongside her, giving her pointers as she went. *"They'll love you out there. You were born to play this part."*

Now? Now, the previous couple of months' work would come to nothing. The auditorium was booked up every weekend over the next month or more. The children in the musical would have other obligations: gymnastics and music lessons and softball and the like. People would move on from *Annie* as though it had never happened. But what was Cora meant to do? Was this really all she got after the bravery of stepping out of her house as a widow?

Cora wandered down the hallway, headed toward a wide window that allowed a gorgeous view of what was poised to be the worst blizzard she'd seen in all her years on the island. Before she reached the window, she paused alongside a collection of photographs from previous performances. Her stomach clenched tight at the sight. She'd forgotten about this, forgotten about the framed photographs of herself and Victor from years past— Tony and Maria in *West Side Story*, Curly and Laurie from *Oklahoma*, Maria and Captain Von Trapp from *The Sound of Music*. The list went on, of course; there were other photographs in other places, lodged away in Cora's old dresser drawer.

Gosh, they'd been young. Cora gazed at a photograph of herself, age twenty-nine, not long after little Madeline had come into this world and then immediately left it behind. You couldn't see that sorrow marred across Cora's face within the photograph. Her face as Maria from *The Sound of Music* echoed with longing and belief in beauty. In many respects, the Cora from back then didn't believe in beauty at all. Not after what time had done to Madeline.

Cora inhaled sharply and closed her eyes. It felt claustrophobic, standing in the auditorium as the snow locked them away for who knew how long. She could practically feel the government workers brimming with fear about what to do next and how to get rid of the snow. Meanwhile, they would probably be stuck at the auditorium for a night or two— eating whatever was in the attached cafeteria, just like Rooster suggested.

A step echoed at the end of the hallway. Cora turned to find Daddy Warbucks' Hank, still dressed in his bald cap. Cora's stomach twisted at the sight. This was to be her private time with her thoughts. She couldn't face him, a man that a small part of her heart had dared to crush on. Yet here he came, his footsteps growing nearer.

"You're still in the bald cap, I see," Cora tried out a joke.

Hank's face widened with laughter. "You don't think it should be a full-time thing?"

"On the contrary, if you still have your hair, shouldn't you celebrate that?"

Hank shrugged. "I think the baldness demands respect." Even still, he lifted a hand and removed the bald cap gently, then swept his hand through his unruly mane. His eyes found the large window as he took in the weight of snow outside. He whistled. "I'm a New Englander through and through, and even this seems like something special to me."

"It's like a sign from God himself," Cora tried.

"That we shouldn't perform the acclaimed musical *Annie?*"

Cora laughed, recognizing how silly she sounded. Maybe everything she'd built up in her mind didn't matter as much as she thought it did.

Hank whistled as he took in the framed photographs of Cora and Victor and the rest of the Vineyard cast hanging on the wall. "Look at you! How old were you here?" He pointed at *The Sound of Music* photograph and arched an eyebrow.

"Twenty-nine," she told him. "It pains me to think what role I would have if we did *The Sound of Music* again. Maybe one of the old nuns..."

Hank shook his head. "No way. You could play anything you wanted to. You're transcendent on stage."

Cora's throat tightened at the compliment. Hank descended farther down the hallway and stopped short in front of the *Fiddler on the Roof* photograph. "I love this one," he explained. "I always watched the musical on television. My ex-wife thought it was insane that I liked it so much. I think she would have preferred that I watch more football."

"I suppose football can be a sort of performance," Cora tried, giving him a small smile.

"Not like *Fiddler on the Roof*," Hank told her pointedly. "That one song... 'Sunrise, Sunset'..." He placed a hand on his heart, closing his eyes as he began to sing it. It turned into a soft and somber chant, his beautiful voice rising and falling.

A moment later, it surprised Cora to realize that she'd joined him in singing. Their voices came together beautifully, harmonizing. During these moments, Cora forgot where she was and how the snow continued to swirl outside, locking them in tightly together. She only knew the sound of her voice, aligning so beautifully with Hank. She only knew the power of music. She only knew this.

After several seconds of this beauty, Cora stopped swiftly, biting her tongue. It was as though she'd suddenly remembered the heaviness of her life. How could she possibly allow herself to shove away any memory of Victor, even as she stood directly in front of their old photographs?

Hank's eyes clouded as he slowly faded out of the song as well. He blinked back at the photographs, clearly seeing the handsome man beside Cora and easily putting two and two together. But instead of mentioning something, instead of demanding something from Cora that she couldn't possibly give, he placed a hand timidly on the back of his neck. He bowed his forehead toward the far corner, nearest the window, where a large vending machine sat, lying in wait.

"I don't know about you, but I get hungry when I'm stressed," Hank told her as he headed for the machine.

Cora followed after him, her heart jumping into her throat. Once at the end of the hall, she leaned her forehead against the sharp chill of the glass. The snow seemed hungry to swallow up the world all at once.

"What do you think?" Hank asked her without turning back to catch her eye. "Milky Way? Snickers? PayDay?"

Cora laughed lightly. "I haven't had a candy bar in like ten years— maybe more."

"What?" This time, Hank did turn around to ogle her.

"I'm fifty-seven, Hank. I can't just stuff a Snickers in my pocket for lunch and call it a day anymore," Cora teased. "I miss that from the old days, though. You always had this sense that your body was your friend, your ally. It all changes so quickly, doesn't it? Your jeans start to tease you for your bad eating habits. Your brain fogs up."

"Listen up, Cora. You can be sad about a lot of things right now. And you have a right to be. But don't ruin my candy habit for me," Hank told her, his grin crooked as he snuck a dollar bill from his wallet.

For not the first time, Cora took in the full breadth of this man, down to the athletic flatness of his stomach. Clearly, whatever he was doing, it was working.

"I would take a couple of bites of a Snickers bar," Cora glanced at him, feigning her annoyance. "But only because we're trapped in this place in the worst blizzard I've ever seen."

Hank and Cora watched in silence as the little coil rotated back and spat the Snickers into the belly of the vending machine below. It was such a simple action, something Cora had witnessed probably more times than she could count. Hank removed the candy bar from the bottom and lifted it, nodding as he slowly peeled back the wrapper and placed it in Cora's hands.

"You haven't had a Snickers in ten years. Do me the honor of taking the first bite."

Cora positioned her teeth tenderly at the very top part of the chocolate bar and bit down slowly, eyeing the snow outside as it swirled mere inches from their heads. A cascading waterfall of caramel and peanut and chocolate met her tongue. The sweetness was overdone and entirely false, but something about it was nourishing, if only because it brought her back to another time. A time she could only get back through memory—a time of youth.

"See?" Hank said as she chewed. He accepted the chocolate bar back and placed his mouth exactly where hers had been moments before. "It's better than you remember it being, isn't it?"

"It's almost revolutionary," Cora agreed. "And I don't even really know why."

Chapter Eighteen

Backstage, the director's office was a cornucopia of memories from the Martha's Vineyard theater troupe's fifty years of history. Only once had Lola dared to piece through the desk, lifting the yellowed newspaper articles and old photographs and silly props from musicals that people didn't even perform any longer. In the wake of her announcement to the cast and crew that the show would not, in fact, continue, Lola collapsed at this very director desk and placed her face in her hands. Amanda and Audrey hustled after her as the cast and crew grew louder and increasingly manic outside.

"Trapped with drama types for who knows how long," Audrey tried on the joke as she clipped the door shut. "What did we do to deserve this?"

Lola rubbed her temples as she tried to piece together her thoughts. Meanwhile, Audrey and Amanda went through their phones, going through the messages they'd received prior to the storm knocking out the service.

"Christine sent me a picture of them all at the Sheridan House," Audrey said. "Little Max, Mia,

Grandpa Wes, and Kellan and Susan..." Audrey's lip bobbed around with sadness. "I hate being away from him for even a few hours. I still have no idea how I moved away to Penn State! What was I thinking?"

"Sam says everyone at the Sunrise Cove is panicked," Amanda told them, reading through her messages as well. "It says that there's a large group there from Louisiana, and they've hardly experienced any type of snow before. He explained to them that this is a really different kind of storm, hence why they call it a blizzard. The kind that might keep them on the island for a few days longer than they'd planned." Amanda then chuckled, drawing a hand over her mouth before she added, "Apparently, the only thing Sam can think of to do for everyone is show them the board game collection and get the servers on staff at the Bistro to serve everyone wine."

"That's one way to get through the blizzard," Lola agreed.

"He's a genius." Amanda smiled to herself as she placed her phone back on the desk alongside an ancient pile of papers.

"Noah's at his mom's place," Audrey reported. "He said she's making enough macaroni and cheese to get them through the next few days."

Lola's stomach groaned spontaneously. "We have to feed everyone soon. It'll calm their nerves. Make it seem more like a party."

"The attached cafeteria has a really tight schedule of events," Amanda reported. "I was looking at the calendar out in the hallway. They just had a big retirement party last night. Two hundred guests. I think we should go investigate the food situation. Prepare some kind of feast, even if it's just leftovers like potato salad and crackers."

"You're such a survivor, Amanda," Audrey teased. "I would love to have you with me on a desert island."

"You joke, but to be honest with you, I've seen almost every survival-themed show, and I think I could make it longer than most," Amanda said as she headed for the door.

"Everyone who watches those survival shows says that," Audrey called as she scampered after her. "But I, for one, have never seen you make a fire from scratch or hunt a wild animal for food. On the other hand, I've watched you pick all the raisins from your granola because you wanted to avoid too many carbs."

Lola's chuckle didn't form any sort of smile across her face. She followed her daughter and niece softly, resolutely, as the reality of the current situation curdled in her belly. Tommy had called her twice prior to her service dying out. What did that mean? Could he leave the mainland and come to the island at all? Was he anywhere near her?

Lola was struck, now, with a thought that nearly took her to the ground.

When she hadn't bothered to be in love with anyone, she'd had a whole lot less to worry about. Now that she'd given her entire romantic heart to Tommy, she felt as though she walked a tightrope that hovered over potential sorrow. One wrong move— one failed sailing expedition or bad freight trip, and Lola would lose the greatest love she'd ever known. With the phones down, her mind was allowed to stew in reckless thoughts of potential tragedies.

It didn't matter that their wedding was probably off for the time being.

It didn't matter that the show wouldn't go on.

The only thing that mattered was holding the ones you loved close to your heart— until they passed. And with all the evils of the world, all the accidents, how could you possibly manage that? Lola was suddenly terrified about Audrey, who'd single-handedly gotten into more personal accidents than nearly any other child Lola had encountered. Still, she'd made it to twenty. But longer?

Lola had never lingered on such sorrowful thoughts before. Ordinarily, she felt too intelligent to be anything but optimistic. She generally felt that optimism was a tool, one that you had to harness to build the life you wanted.

Suddenly, Audrey appeared wide-eyed before her. "Mom? You okay?"

Lola whacked her head left and right, clearing the cobwebs between her ears. "Sorry, I was just lost in my own thoughts for a moment. Spiraling like crazy."

Audrey arched an eyebrow as she laced her fingers through her mother's right hand. Lola was genuinely certain that her daughter had never seen Lola look so petrified, like a boat without an anchor. How could Lola express the terror of falling in love for the first time at forty? How could she possibly tell her daughter how weak she was?

"I'm really sorry, Mom," Audrey murmured gently as they walked toward the cafeteria. "I don't even know what to say. I'm just really sorry."

"Being sorry for the weather is the silliest thing of all, isn't it?" Lola finally told her, drawing the strength from somewhere within her heart. She squeezed her daughter's hand a tiny bit harder and forced a smile, one that almost felt natural after only a split second.

They found Amanda beneath the sterile fluorescent lights in the cafeteria's kitchen, going through large basins of what looked to be last night's recently refrigerated dinner.

"Chili con carne and chili sin carne!" Amanda cried as they entered. "It's the perfect food to go around. And I found some mix for cornbread in the cabinet. We can have a big feast in the cafeteria in probably about an hour."

"And how about tomorrow?" Lola asked as she stepped toward the fridge.

"Look for yourself," Amanda told her excitedly, showing off her survivor mentality. "There are eggs, cheese, milk, and sausages, enough to feed probably fifty people. I think they planned to have some kind of breakfast for the sailing club tomorrow morning. Luckily, they brought the supplies early."

Audrey tiptoed toward the farthest closet on the other side of the enormous cafeteria stove. There, she opened the gleaming white door to find a selection of drinks, including sodas, juices, and several bottles of wine, probably forgotten after a recent retirement dinner or birthday party. Audrey whipped around and clapped her hands excitedly.

"I think we should make tonight a real party," Audrey suggested with a wide grin. "If we can't perform for the masses, we might as well eat, drink, and be merry all together."

"Don't give the kids too much soda, though," Amanda warned. "Kids that are hopped up on sugar drive me nuts."

* * *

Two and a half hours later, the theater kids banded together after a bountiful feast of both meat and vegetarian chilis, plus delectable cornbread and buckets of wine and soda. They somehow took control of the soda pop machines and ultimately did precisely what Amanda had prayed they wouldn't: they drank their weight in sugary pop and grew wide-eyed and very nearly insane.

That said, the adults weren't exactly on their best behavior, either. Audrey had brought out all the wine bottles and served everyone from Miss Hannigan to Rooster to Daddy Warbucks and beyond. Midway through his second glass of wine, Daddy Warbucks disappeared to check the snowfall and returned to announce that it seemed like it was coming down at a rate of two or three inches per hour— something generally unheard of in New England.

With the hubbub that followed, Lola felt an urge to calm everyone down. She stood on her cafeteria stool and clacked her knife against the edge of her wineglass. Slowly, the sugar-ed children and the panicked-looking adults quieted and turned their attention to Lola.

"Well. Thank you. Thank you, everyone, for your attention," Lola began. "We've found ourselves in quite a unique situation, haven't we?"

"You can say that again," Cecily, the overly loud costume director called.

Lola sighed. "I could dwell about how sad I am about all of this— about missing opening night after working so hard or about missing our family and friends." Lola's eyes continued to scan down the line of the theater cast and crew until she stumbled across Cora and Hank, who sat very close to one another— so much so that their shoulders nearly touched.

"But I don't want to feel sad," Lola explained reso-lutely. "And if there's anything I've learned from all of you artistic folks, it's that all you need to do in life is fake it till you make it. Tonight, I suggest we drink soda or wine or whatever it is that makes you happy, head to the auditorium, and have a talent show! It'll distract us from the rest of the world and get us exhausted and ready for bed later. It'll certainly beat moping about our current situation. Our lovely assistant director, Amanda, found a number of pillows and blankets in a supply closet, and we will be making a cozy sleeping area right on stage after we crown the talent show king or queen. How does that sound to all of you?"

In the wake of Lola's speech, the mood shifted from panic and anxiety to one of unbridled joy. Hurriedly, the cast and crew prepared an assembly line to clean the dishes, put away the rest of the chili, and refill the drinks. Each prepared a talent in their minds and talked about it wildly, seemingly without hearing whoever they spoke to talk about theirs in return.

"I'll do a dance number I've been practicing," one twelve-year-old girl who had been dying to play Annie recited to a friend.

"I have my guitar in the back room," Rooster said. "I'll do a Bob Dylan cover."

"I can do my magic show!"

"I'll do my gymnastics routine!"

One after another, the theater troupe bustled back toward the auditorium, leaving in their wake a spotless cafeteria. Amanda refilled her glass of wine and eyed Lola mischievously.

"I see you're the morale booster of the survival team," she told her.

"I didn't know that was a thing on a desert island," Lola returned, grinning at her niece.

"Oh yes," Amanda affirmed.

Audrey groaned to herself as they headed back to the auditorium to join them. "I don't want to perform."

"Aud, don't be silly," Amanda said. "We're obviously the judges of the talent show."

"Oh. Sitting around, drinking wine and being judgmental?" Audrey's eyes shone with excitement.

"I know. It's all you really like to do," Amanda affirmed. "It's perfect for you."

Over the following two hours, the Martha's Vineyard theater troupe performed a collection of numbers— everything from group dances to acoustic guitar-backed solos to Shakespearean monologues. As they were theater people through and through, they took the task of a talent show incredibly serious and bowed deeply after each performance. Lola, Audrey, and Amanda took diligent notes and discussed each performance honestly, noting its strengths and weaknesses.

When Cora and Hank stood on stage together, Lola's heart quickened with curiosity. There seemed to be a strange energy that simmered between the two of them. To her surprise, Cora bent toward the microphone and announced that she and Hank would perform an old tune they'd both learned they liked, titled "Take the Long Way Home" by Supertramp. Hank whipped a guitar out before him, balancing it tenderly across his stomach and strumming it confidently. When they began to sing the old seventies tune, their voices joined together in beautiful synchronicity. It was as though they'd practiced side by side like this for years.

Cora's face was alight throughout the entire performance, exhibiting emotions Lola hadn't perceived within Cora's bruised and battered soul.

When they finished, Lola, Audrey, and Amanda ducked their heads together to whisper.

"Cora and Hank are amazing together. And hot," Audrey breathed.

"Not everyone has to be hot together, Aud," Amanda pointed out. "Maybe they're just friends."

"There's no way they're just friends. You could cut that sexual tension with a knife," Audrey stated.

Amanda rolled her eyes back toward Lola, who sat in stunned silence.

"What?" Audrey demanded.

"Sorry, I'm just thinking about the day they auditioned for their parts," Lola explained. "They both seemed like the loneliest people in the world. And just now..."

"They looked like they belonged. If not together, then to the group at large," Amanda finished Lola's sentence. "I feel that, too. Like they really needed this."

"I think maybe we all did," Lola breathed. "For different reasons."

Lola, Audrey, and Amanda announced the top three awards for what they called "The First Annual Snowed-In Martha's Vineyard Talent Show." They gave the little girl's gymnastic routine third place, Cora and Hank second place, and little Jenny (Annie) first for her near-perfect song and dance routine to the song "Mamma Mia" by ABBA. It was such a surprise to see their little orphan Annie sing with a boisterous and silly voice, dancing around on her little yet powerful legs.

After the talent show, the adults bustled around to set up pillows and blankets for their first overnight as a snowed-in family. Already, the over-sugared soda had pushed the children over the edge. They crashed left and right, with some of them hardly getting under their blankets before drool crept along their chins.

"Good night, everyone!" Lola called out as she headed for backstage, where she, Audrey, and Amanda planned to sleep in the office space. "I'll see you in the morning. And remember what Annie says. The sun will come out tomorrow, so we gotta hang on till tomorrow!"

In the far corner of the stage, Cora and Hank wrapped themselves tightly in thick blankets and curled toward one another as they whispered to each other like children. Lola's ear craned for some sign of what they said. But as she drew closer to backstage, Amanda turned off the lights overhead, casting everything in sinister shadows. It was time to sleep.

Chapter Nineteen

At seven thirty the following morning, Lola stood with a mug of steaming coffee. She gazed up at the impenetrable mound of bright white snow piled against the glass window of the backstage hallway. The very top line of the snow glowed with morning sunlight, proof that the storm clouds had dumped all they could upon them and left a blue sky in their wake. Still, there would be no appreciating the glory of a winter's sun. Not from within the walls of the auditorium. Not until Oak Bluffs sent out its crew of snowplows and got them out.

"Wow." Audrey's voice groaned sleepily from behind Lola as she crept down the hallway to join her. "Look at that."

"It's really something, isn't it?" Lola turned to greet Audrey, whose black makeup streaked down her cheek, flirting with her top lip.

Lola rubbed her thumb across the black streaks as Audrey erupted with a yawn.

"Yeah, yeah. I'm sure I'm a mess," Audrey said sleepily. "Amanda's already down in the cafeteria inspecting the breakfast situation."

"She really is a mini-Susan, isn't she?"

"She might be even worse," Audrey returned with a laugh. "Only time will tell. Can you imagine when Amanda has a baby, though? She probably won't let anyone near the baby with a ten-foot pole. Not until they've been tested for all diseases and washed their hands for thirty minutes."

"Yet she just slept on a dusty floor of the backstage of the theater," Lola pointed out.

"She contains multitudes," Audrey said.

Suddenly, Lola's phone buzzed in her pocket. She reached for it as Audrey's, too, buzzed in her sweatshirt pocket. The service had returned, and with it, Audrey and Lola received a number of missed phone calls and text messages, all from family members and close friends.

CHRISTINE: Hey, honey. I know the service is out. Just thinking of you and missing you and hoping this text message will get to you soon.

CHARLOTTE: Ugh, Lola! This is a disaster, isn't it? Twenty-five of your guests have emailed to say that they can't get to the island in time for the wedding. The storm knocked out so much of the East Coast.

SUSAN: Love you, Lola! I wish you were here, cozy with us. Max misses his grandmother. (I know you hate the term grandmother.)

DAD: Image: A bright red cardinal.

161

DAD: He's back! I couldn't believe it. He arrived this morning and hovered on a branch outside the second-story window. He survived the storm!

Lola chuckled inwardly and then continued through her text messages, only to discover that Tommy hadn't sent her a single text. Her heart dropped into her stomach. Was there something wrong?

"Did Grandpa send you a picture of the bird he's obsessed with?" Audrey asked.

Lola nodded, half sharing a smile as she dialed Tommy's number. The call went directly to voicemail. Where on earth was he?

Without his answer, Lola dialed Susan. Her heart thudded in her throat.

"Lola! L-O-L-A! Lola!" Susan called out the lyrics to the old song by The Kinks as she answered joyfully. "The phones are back, I see!"

"Yes. I just got all of your messages. Have you managed to get back to your house yet? Or are you still at Dad's?"

"We're all at Dad's place right now," Susan replied. "Except for Scott, and I still haven't heard from him." There it was: a hint of fear edging along her words.

"Gosh, I'm sorry. That's one of the reasons I called you. Tommy was supposed to come back to the island on one of the Frampton freights. I haven't heard anything from him, and his phone seems to be off."

"Scott's is off, too," Susan groaned.

Lola dropped her head back as worry permeated through her. "I don't know what to do." Her voice broke. "We're supposed to get married tomorrow."

And now, she didn't even know if he was safe...

"Listen, honey. If there's one thing I know, it's that Tommy and Scott are very strong and capable men," Susan told her, seeming to know that she needed to step up and be the courageous sister. "They're fine. They probably just forgot their phone chargers. That's not exactly Scott's strong suit."

"Tommy's not great at remembering his charger, either," Lola admitted. "Still, I wish they'd contact us."

"It's a weird time," Susan affirmed. "But we're in a warm place, and we have food and water and shelter. I'm sure Tommy and Scott are somewhere warm and safe as well, and maybe they're even together."

* * *

Around nine, the theater troupe banded together to eat Amanda's cheesy-gooey egg casserole, drink coffee, and talk about the night's talent show event as though it had been the performance of the season. Nearly everyone's phones had gotten service back, which meant that every child had been able to call his or her parents and report their safety.

"Yes, Mom. I'm well-fed. Yes, Mom. I'm warm. Yes, Mom. I'm behaving myself," a little girl said in a bored tone as she swung her legs beneath the cafeteria stool.

"My mom says hi." This was Rachel, who appeared before Lola, Audrey, and Amanda and grinned excitedly. Her hair had been braided into several different and sloppy cornrows. Abby and Gail hopped up on either side of her, sporting similar hairdos. Probably, they'd found a little corner of the auditorium for a sleepover all their own and had whispered long into the night as they braided one another's hair. This would be a memory for the ages.

"How is she doing?" Lola asked.

"She's pretty upset that your wedding won't go through," Rachel admitted.

"What a sweetie. She worked so hard for me," Lola said with a sigh. "And your momma, Gail? Abby?"

"She's good," Abby recited. "She was worried sick, but now that she knows we're okay, I think she's just glad we're out of the house for a few days."

"She's counting down the days till we go to college," Gail affirmed.

"I don't think that's true at all," Lola told them. "Your mom won't know what hit her when you two run off the island."

The three teenage girls shrugged into a group giggle and then sped back to their table, where they tore through another helping of breakfast biscuits and gossiped about whatever it was that teenage girls gossiped about.

"I was just that age," Audrey stated, her eyebrows lifting. "But I think when I had Max, something changed, and I can't speak that language anymore. Speaking of which..." Audrey grabbed her phone to bring up another photograph Christine had sent of little Max, who was now three hundred and sixty-four days old. "I can't believe it. My little man, all grown up."

"Almost one year on the planet." Amanda slid some butter across her biscuit with a plastic knife. "And to think. He won't remember the drama of his birthday at all."

"Christine says we'll have a birthday party when we're all back home," Audrey said. "She was going to make the birthday cake yesterday but held off."

"Looks like she just made mounds of croissants instead." Amanda flashed a photograph from Susan of the breakfast table at the Sheridan House, making them all groan with jealousy.

"I'd give anything to be there," Lola confessed.

"Sam reports that the plows have begun to dig the town out," Amanda affirmed. "But who knows how long that will take?"

"Certainly not as long as it will take the Sheridan crew to eat all those croissants," Audrey admitted. "I have half a mind to dig out of this auditorium myself."

"What will you do once you're out there? Snowshoe to the Sheridan House?" Amanda teased.

Audrey grumbled. "I don't know. The only thing I know is that I've seen *The Shining*. And people don't act nicely when they're trapped inside due to snow for very long."

"We can keep everyone sane for another day," Lola said as she scraped her plate. She then snapped her fingers as an idea came over her. She jumped onto the stool and quieted the cast before her as she announced her plan.

"It's looking like we'll be trapped inside another day at least..." Lola announced. "But I've thought of a great way to pass the time. We all know the musical *Annie* backward and forward by now, don't we?"

"Yes..." The cast eyed one another curiously.

"I think everyone should swap parts," Lola suggested, looking out into the crowd before her. "Throw caution to the wind. Cora, you'll play Annie. Hank, you're Rooster instead of Daddy Warbucks. Jenny, you're Miss Hannigan instead of Annie." One after another, Lola assigned different parts to an excited batch of actors, all of whom couldn't wait to sink their teeth into another role for one performance and one performance only.

"What should we wear for costumes?" Jenny cried as she scrambled past.

"Anything you want to!" Lola told her. "Anything you find in the back room is yours to wear in any way you choose. I'm sure Cecily can help you figure something out."

Because it was a one-time performance and a very strange one at that, most everyone took their scripts out on stage to ensure they got their lines down. Jenny was all-out hilarious as Miss Hannigan, sauntering across the stage like an angry, arrogant woman instead of a little girl. Hank was excellent as Rooster, getting almost all of the song and dance numbers down as he and Jenny fell in cahoots to take advantage of Annie and get Daddy Warbucks's cash.

Most notably, of course, with hardly a glance at the script, Cora knew nearly every single line that Annie said throughout the musical and absolutely nailed every single song. Despite her fifty-seven years, she matched the innocence and the sorrow of a youthful orphan Annie, and her solos were absolutely electric, mesmerizing every other person in the cast.

After a particularly wonderful solo, Cora's eyes filled with tears as she suddenly broke character. When the scene ended, she whirled around to find Hank beside her, his eyes alight with wonder. Lola's heart shattered as she watched Cora step into his arms, shaking with what seemed to be a strange mix of emotions. Hank held her while she shook, becoming her anchor to the world even as her thoughts took her somewhere far, far away.

"Gosh, that was intense," Audrey whispered into Lola's ear as Hank and Cora slowly walked off the stage.

"They certainly have a relationship all their own,"

Amanda added. "It's like this in every survivor movie. There's always a romance."

"You and your survivor movies," Audrey said. "You know, I wonder if they'll point to this time in the auditorium as the time when they realized they're in love..."

"You think this storm changed the course of history?" Amanda rasped.

"Absolutely," Audrey affirmed. "It canceled my mother's wedding, eliminated Jenny's debut as Annie, made us all realize Amanda's two steps away from being a prepper, and brought the unlikely duo of Cora and Hank together. Wake up, Amanda. We're living history."

Chapter Twenty

Saturday night, as Cora curled beneath a thick winter blanket in the far corner of the shadowed stage, she turned to face Hank, mere inches off to the left, and whispered, "I've never slept this close to anyone before." Of course, what she meant was that she'd never slept this close to anyone except her husband before. Hank's expression was difficult to read. He reached across the space between them and drew a line across her palm with his thumb. The motion was so tender, so unexpected, that Cora's heart nearly shattered with surprise. Instead of allowing her words to fade away into nothingness, Hank whispered back, "Neither have I." Both of them knew that, at their age, they came off decades of human experience, of heartache. But there was something so beautiful, so youthful, so alive about spending these nights locked away in the downtown auditorium. Cora had always believed in the magic of theater. Perhaps it had far more magic up its sleeves than she'd bargained for.

She almost prayed for another day latched away but

held the prayers back. The children were beginning to miss their parents, and the food supply would soon run out. The hazy in-between of this time couldn't last forever. She would, very soon, return to her house alone.

When she awoke the following morning, Hank continued to sleep peacefully beside her. She had a strange urge to lean over, to kiss his cheek, but she instead lifted herself up and headed backstage to find a bathroom. Once there, she witnessed the glorious heavenly light of the fresh morning, which crept up over the top of what looked like almost five feet of snow that pressed against the large glass door at the far end of the hallway. This was where Hank had bought that Snickers and started a strangely romantic story for them both— one that Cora would certainly return to in her mind as the years went by. *Remember it forever. You'll need it during your sad and lonely nights.*

As Cora studied the large glass door, their only exit to a world that no longer existed for them, there came the sound of footsteps behind her. Cora froze as her heart leaped, praying for the footfalls to reveal themselves as Hank's. How addicted she'd gotten.

But instead, when she turned back, she found Lola carrying a mug of steaming coffee. Her long hair streamed wildly down her back after two days without showering. Her eyes were without makeup, and crow's feet crept toward her hairline when she smiled. Still, she smiled, sharing a tender moment with Cora at the edge of their little auditorium world.

"Are you feeling claustrophobic yet?" Lola asked, leaning against the wall.

Cora shrugged lightly. "The only person who makes me feel claustrophobic is myself, I think." She tapped the side of her head. "More often, I'm circling through the same thoughts as I sit alone in my house. At least this has allowed me to examine my life and have some new thoughts."

"That's an interesting perspective." Lola pushed off the wall and crept closer to the glass door, pressing her hand against the chill of the glass morosely.

"Any word on what's happening out there?" Cora asked.

Lola shook her head. "As of last night, Amanda's boyfriend said that they hadn't cleared a path all the way to the Sunrise Cove yet, but they're close. That probably means we're next. Fingers crossed."

The two women stood in silence, gazing at the sharp light over the top of the pile of snow. The light looked like icing, overly sugared and bright over the cake of the snow. Lola stepped back, took a sip, and then asked Cora a question that surprised her so much that it took her outside of herself for a moment.

"I've been so curious. Thinking about the decisions we make, all without knowing what will happen next. We're like fools, aren't we? Making plans for a future that might never happen."

Cora knew that Lola referred to her planned marriage with that sailor, Tommy Gasbarro. She felt the density of her fears.

"So I guess my question is, knowing what you know now about what happened to you, would you take any of it back?" Lola breathed. "After all you've been through?"

Cora blinked furiously as tears threatened to fall. She hadn't any idea what to do with her hands. Flashing images of her life with Victor came through her. But before she thought about it a moment more, the answer fell onto her tongue.

"I wouldn't take a single day back," she answered firmly. "I loved every minute of my time with Victor. Even if we'd only been given five minutes of time together, I'd still do it all over again."

Lola nodded and dropped her chin toward her chest. The clock on the wall read seven fifty-seven. Time ticked evermore toward some impossible future that they couldn't name. Lola swiped her hand beneath her eye to mop up a tear.

"I suppose we should get back to the others," Lola suggested. "Amanda's already planning out the breakfast for the morning. And I can hear the girls singing away in there. Always so much energy to sing."

As Lola and Cora turned back to face the belly of the auditorium, a strange, scraping noise came from just outside the door. The shadows around the hallway shifted, alternating sides as the snow behind them changed. Cora froze with surprise as Lola whipped around.

"There's a shovel! Oh my gosh! Someone's shoveling us out!" Lola rushed toward the door as Cora hung back, her heart quickening with a mix of sorrow and excitement.

A shovel whipped along the top of the snow and shoveled the white fluff up and over. Bit by bit, two large figures dressed in several layers of clothing appeared between the two thick walls of snow. From where Cora stood, it seemed they'd shovel a fifteen-foot path all the way from the parking lot to the auditorium door.

With a vibrant rush of energy, Lola grabbed the door and pushed it open just as one of two of the men tore off his hat to reveal luscious black locks and bright eyes of adoration.

"Tommy!" Lola cried as she jumped into his arms.

Tommy, her fiancé, stepped into the hallway with Lola in his wet and frigid arms. It seemed she didn't care at all. He whipped her around and around in circles so that her legs extended out behind her. Her squeals echoed out across the halls and into the auditorium itself.

The other man stepped through the door and greeted Lola with a side hug. When he removed his hat, Cora recognized him as Susan Sheridan's husband, Scott Frampton.

"You two! You're in big trouble. Why haven't you answered any of my texts or calls?" Lola demanded with a mix of exasperation and joy.

"We left our chargers in Boston," Scott explained. "It was such a rush getting back onto the island. And then, once we got here early this morning, we were recruited to deal with the snow."

"We did our best to get over here as soon as we could," Tommy affirmed. "Figured you were going crazy in here with the entire cast and crew of *Annie* on what was supposed to be our wedding day."

Lola blushed and flung herself forward to kiss Tommy directly on the lips. When she stepped back, she blinked back tears and gestured over to Cora, introducing her.

"This is my dear friend, Cora," Lola introduced softly. "Since the snow buried us all in here together, she's given me tremendous insights on life. I only hope to take her wisdom along with me as I grow older."

Cora winked back at her as her throat tightened with sorrow. Just behind them, several cast and crew members gathered, brought there by the sharp chill from the door and Lola's screaming. Amanda and Audrey hustled forward to greet both Tommy and Scott warmly, with Amanda throwing her arms around her stepfather's shoulders and howling, "Oh my gosh. Scott! You saved us!"

Tommy and Lola hovered toward the side of the hallway as the cast and crew rushed back to gather their things and bundle up to go outside. Cora could just make out their whispered words as Lola explained that twenty-five of their guests wouldn't be able to make it to the island anyway, that maybe summertime was a better bet for the wedding of their dreams. "Maybe we can even sail off toward the sunset after our reception, like in the movies," Lola whispered, still blinking back tears.

Suddenly, Hank appeared in the hallway, carrying all of his and Cora's things. He smiled sheepishly and assisted her in slipping her coat over her shoulders. Cora briefly lost track of what Lola and Tommy whispered to one another. She felt herself in a story all her own.

"Why don't we take a walk outside?" Hank suggested. "See if we can make it home."

Cora wanted to tell him, at that moment, how she felt about him— how he'd become the most blissful surprise. But instead, she replied, "That sounds good. I have to admit that I'm a little worried about my plants. I can't remember the last time I watered them."

At this, Hank chuckled as though he knew how much she cared and how little she knew how to show it. "Let's get you home to water those plants, then. Lola? We cleared to go?"

Lola smiled and waved a hand from just behind Tommy's burly frame. "Thank you for everything, you two. I'll be here a little while longer to make sure everyone has a way home. Have fun out there. Enjoy the winter wonderland."

Cora and Hank walked through the strange air of the dug-out path and then burst into the sterling brightness of the mostly plowed parking lot. Enormous walls of snow lifted high on either side of the lot and the downtown streets, giving no space yet for sidewalks. That would come later.

Meanwhile, Cora and Hank walked quietly along the edge of the empty road. A plow fought against snow a half mile down the road, tearing it to one side of the street. Cora's home was rather close in walking distance, so she felt positive about her ability to return.

"Looks like they haven't cleared my street yet," Hank said after a few minutes more, pointing down a side street that remained a mountain of white.

"Oh, dear." Cora's heart jumped into her throat. Would she really ask this man over to her home? Did she have a choice? "Well, you can come to my place for a little while."

Hank smiled. "I can help you water those plants."

Cora's cheeks burned red with embarrassment. Hopefully, he assumed the red cheeks were proof of how cold she was and nothing more.

Luckily, Cora's next-door neighbor, Henrietta's husband, who had a snowplow of his own, had plowed her driveway, which allowed Cora to step directly up to the garage door and type in the code.

"Wow. You had angels watching out for you," Hank pointed out.

"They feel bad for their widowed neighbor," Cora said without thinking. She then shrugged, choosing not to apologize for her words. "Sometimes, the pity gets old.

But today, I am grateful for it. I'll make them some cookies or something to say thanks. That's what a sad little widow would do, right?"

Once within Cora's home, Hank clicked the door closed and took in the sights of her quaint ecosystem. The plants, as advertised, were gloriously jungle-like, their leaves stretching toward the sky. A photograph of Victor hung off to the left, focused in a practical wooden frame. Cora removed her coat and headed for the kitchen, where she began to boil hot water for tea.

"For the record," Hank started as he removed his own coat. "I don't think of you as a sad little widow at all. And I don't think anyone else does, either. At least, not anyone who's gotten to know you properly."

Cora stared down at the kettle, which grew angry with the heat below it. "I didn't imagine I'd ever want someone to know me properly again."

Hank leaned in the doorway between the kitchen and the dining room. On the day after Victor's death, Cora had slept with her head on the dining room table, still in the clothes that she'd been wearing when she found him. Nobody else had been inside her home since Victor's death. No one except the handyman who'd fixed the washing machine six months ago and her neighbor, Henrietta, when she pushed her way through.

"Cora..." Hank began, sounding unsure of himself.

Cora's instincts screamed at her to tell him to leave her alone. *I don't have the space in my heart for something like this. I can't manage to feel anything for you. I cannot be your second wife. I can hardly be anyone's friend.*

Suddenly, Hank's phone buzzed in his coat pocket. He fished it out begrudgingly as though he hadn't wanted to budge from the conversation at hand. As he read the message, his eyes nearly bugged out of his head.

"What is it?"

"I can't believe it. I can't believe she made it."

"Who?" Cora demanded.

"My daughter..." Hank's incredulity made him shake his head. "She's on the island. I told her about the musical and never imagined in a million years she'd come. She and I, we haven't gotten along much since the divorce."

A daughter. Hank had a daughter. A daughter who loved him, despite the mess of the life he'd left behind.

"And she's never come to the island, although I've always wanted her to see it. She decided to surprise me but then was trapped in Woods Hole until this morning. Since she'd come all this way before the storm, she decided to see how far she could make it. She just checked in to the Sunrise Cove Inn and wants to see me."

Overwhelmed with the joy that reflected back through Hank's eyes, Cora suddenly walked over and embraced him. As the kettle squealed behind her, Cora placed her chin on Hank's shoulder, closed his eyes, and inhaled the beautiful density of this moment. Just as she and Lola had said, there was no telling what came next.

But you had to live, dammit. You had to live as well as you could and feel as much as you could possibly feel. Perhaps Hank was her answer to that.

"Come with me," Hank told her as their hug broke.

"I couldn't. It sounds like this is a very special moment for you two."

Hank shook his head ever so slightly. "I want you there, Cora. We've been through a lot together the past few days. I don't want this to end just yet."

Chapter Twenty-One

After Tommy's spontaneous and heroic shoveling through the snow to save Lola from the auditorium, he and Scott sped off to shovel more sidewalks and assist the town of Oak Bluffs on clambering out from beneath the soft white, very thick blanket. Just before he left, Tommy kissed Lola tenderly and told her, "I'll see you later today. Don't be a stranger."

According to a text from Sam, the road from the auditorium to the Sunrise Cove Inn was now "more plowed than not," which led Audrey to pack her things and rush out. "I have to try to make it home," she explained as she reached for the door. "It's Max's first birthday! I don't want to miss any more time than I already have!"

Amanda, the ever-responsible one, stayed behind with Lola to ensure that the children of the theater troupe were able to get back home. One after another, parents arrived on foot, in massive trucks, or on snowmobiles, anxious to wrap their children with strong-armed hugs and bring them back to the warmth and safety of their houses across Oak Bluffs. Those who lived in Edgartown or other surrounding communities found refuge with friends in Oak Bluffs. Lola watched with bated breath as parents who could get there called up parents who couldn't and explained the situation in greater detail.

"I can take her. Don't worry about it," one mother offered over the phone.

"I'll get some good and healthy lunch in her before you come by," another mother said. "Even dinner."

"She can sleep over for as long as she wants."

As Charlotte and Claire were both still trapped in their houses, Lola gathered up Rachel, Gail, and Abby, who were midway through learning yet another dance to yet another pop song, and tugged them out of the auditorium and back toward the Sunrise Cove. As they approached the inn, a large Oak Bluffs plow swept toward them, clearing the road between the Sunrise Cove and the Sheridan House. As it went, Audrey leaped out of the Sunrise Cove, waving a hand as she took off down the road to meet her baby boy.

"There she goes," Lola said with a laugh.

"This is where I part ways," Amanda announced. "I'll see you back at home later." With that, Amanda struck up toward the front of the Sunrise Cove, where Sam awaited her, his arms outstretched. She flung herself into his arms as he lifted her, twirling her in a big circle.

When Lola turned back, she found Rachel, Gail, and Abby in almost comedic formation, watching Amanda with bugged eyes. Lola could feel the teenagers' adoration for this moment. How romantic teenage girls were! How they craved to meet the love of their lives, even at fifteen, sixteen, seventeen! Lola wished she could bottle that feeling, one that convinced her anything was possible as long as she was in love.

"Come on, girls. Amanda will meet us back at home," Lola said.

Slowly, she dragged Rachel, Gail, and Abby back down the road for the ten-minute walk to the home where she'd grown up. It was nearly eleven o'clock, and the sunshine was as bright as ever. She was confident that everything would turn out just right. Abby, Gail, and Rachel practically skipped back to the Sheridan House, walking that strange line between girlhood and adulthood and unsure where they belonged.

"Hello?" Lola called as she opened the back door into the mudroom.

"Mom! Look!" Audrey appeared with Max in her arms, her eyes lined with tears. On the other side of her, the living room and dining area were decorated with bright blue balloons and streamers. A large banner hung over the top of the room that read: **HAPPY 1ˢᵗ BIRTH-DAY, MAX!**

Lola stumbled out of her boots and coat before she rushed for her daughter and grandson. She wrapped them in a warm hug as Christine and Susan jumped out of the kitchen to greet her. Typical of Max, he seemed very much in tune with the fact that all the attention was meant for him. He excitedly smacked his hands as Audrey showed him the beautiful birthday cake Christine had baked. He even lifted a finger out as far as he could to attempt to slide it across the icing, but Audrey brought him back just in time.

"We thought that, well..." Susan shrugged and glanced toward Christine.

"If we couldn't celebrate your wedding, then we had to celebrate something," Christine affirmed. "I baked the cake last night when we had a hunch that the snow would be plowed enough to get you out of there."

"Baby Max is one! Baby Max is one!" Audrey sing-songed, which resulted in Rachel, Gail, and Abby giving her a disgruntled, teenage look. Audrey laughed outright and said, "You can just tell me I'm not cool anymore, girls. I don't mind. I gave up on being cool when I brought a baby into the world."

"Hello? Is anyone here?" Noah made his way through the back door carrying a big bouquet and a bright-blue balloon. His smile was meant for Audrey and baby Max only, and it seemed he hardly noticed anyone else in the room. After removing his coat, he kissed Max on the fore-head, then Audrey on the lips.

If anyone had seen them without knowing who they were, they would have just assumed that Noah was Max's father. And in fact, Max even looked at him with love and adoration— the way a baby might look at his father.

"It's good to see you," Audrey murmured.

"What a wild few days," Noah agreed as he slowly lifted Max out of Audrey's arms. "Grab yourself a piece of cake. I know how much you like sweets for breakfast."

Audrey cackled. "Not just for breakfast. For every meal."

"Your momma's never going to grow up, is she?" Noah said to Max.

"Hush, you. Don't teach him bad things about me," Audrey teased.

Grandpa Wes stepped into the dining area from the back porch. His binoculars danced across his chest as he greeted Audrey, Lola, Rachel, Gail, and Abby. "My thes-pians are back home! We were worried about you."

"We had Amanda on our side," Audrey explained.

"Grandpa, I had no idea, but she takes after you. She's very resourceful— a complete survivor."

Grandpa Wes considered this stoically. "That is good information to have, Audrey. I suppose I'll take Amanda with me on all my adventures from now on."

After a light breakfast of eggs and toast, Christine slid a candle into the center of Max's birthday cake and lit the tip. Together, everyone sang "Happy Birthday" to a little Max, who bounced outrageously in his mother's arms. With the help of Noah, Audrey leaned forward so that she and Noah could blow out the candle and "hint" that Max had helped as well. Everyone cheered excitedly as the flame extinguished.

Susan cut the cake and slid plates into birthday revelers' hands. With cream cheese frosting and raspberry jam sandwiched between the cake layers, the cake was decadent, and something only Christine Sheridan could have come up with. Max ate a tiny bit and then flung it toward Audrey's chest, dousing it with icing.

"Thanks, little man," Audrey told him playfully. "I'd do anything for you, and this is how you repay me?"

"And it's only the first year," Susan warned.

Throughout the afternoon and early evening, everyone in the house received updates regarding news from the outer world. Scott and Tommy continued to work tirelessly, digging out older residents of Oak Bluffs and ensuring that nobody got plowed in. Finally, Claire arrived to pick up the rowdy teenage girls, who were, by then, over-sugared from Max's birthday cake and singing their renditions of old pop songs. When they disappeared through the snow, Grandpa Wes breathed a sigh of relief.

"My three girls were never as loud as those three girls..." he commented.

Susan laughed and insisted that the Sheridan sisters had had their boisterous days as well. "You just choose to remember the good days, Dad."

"I refuse to believe that," Grandpa Wes countered. "You three were perfect every single day of your lives."

Just past five in the afternoon, Susan disappeared for a few minutes and returned wearing a black dress and a pair of tights. She shoved her feet into her boots and then called out to them, "I just have to run a few errands outside. I'll be back in a jiffy." She then disappeared through the pink haze of the snow-filled evening.

"Where's she going?" Lola asked Christine.

Christine shrugged flippantly and then returned her attention to little Mia, who alternated between little frowns and what looked to be near smiles, although it was far too early for something like that.

A little while later, Audrey and Noah decided to head out on a walk of their own. They bundled Max up and called out their goodbyes from the mudroom.

"You want company?" Lola called.

"We're good!" Audrey returned.

A few minutes later, Zach arrived to pick Christine and Mia up. Their reunion was beautiful if brief. "We better get a move on," Christine said. "Dad? You coming?"

"Going where?" Lola demanded.

"Oh, um. Dad says he wants to help us with a job back at the house," Christine explained timidly. "Zach and I have worked in kitchens our whole lives, and we don't know anything about, um... bathroom plumbing."

"You should ask Scott about that," Lola returned.

"Dad said he'd help. Anyway, we'll see you later?" Christine nearly leaped for the door, leaving Lola in a strange huff in the kitchen before Max's half-eaten birthday cake.

As the door closed, Lola collected the dirty plates and forks and began to scrub everything in the sink. The house seemed enormous around her, creaking against the severity of the winter wind. Lola couldn't remember the last time she'd been alone in the house where she'd grown up. Their memories, their ghosts, seemed extra heavy without the welcome distraction of Max's squeals or the ding of Christine's baking timer. Even her father was gone, hovering over some pipe at Christine's house, pretending he knew a thing or two about plumbing.

This was supposed to be the day of Lola's wedding.

The day when she and Tommy stood up in front of the people they cared for the most and professed their undying love for one another.

But instead, Lola would spend the night beneath an afghan, flicking through TV stations and waiting for the rest of her family to return home. It was almost a sure bet that the roads weren't cleared all the way out to her cabin. Perhaps she would sleep at the Sheridan House alone.

Suddenly, there was a knock on the back door. Lola jumped from the couch on high alert, her heart in her throat. The knock terrified her. Nobody ever knocked on the Sheridan House door. It was an ever-swinging door, a welcoming path for every Martha's Vineyard resident.

"Hello?" Lola called.

Again, the knock.

Slowly, Lola tiptoed toward the back door as her heart slammed against her rib cage. When she'd been a girl, she'd adored scary movies, but those nightmares that had collected on-screen made her especially frightened of the silly creaks and noises of her normal house.

"Hello?"

When Lola reached the door, she saw nothing but the outline of a broad-shouldered man. Soft snow had begun to fall again, mere sprinkles when compared to the monster snowflakes of the previous few days. It was beautiful, soulful, and quiet— the sort of dark winter night that made you think about your life and what you really wanted.

Lola opened the back door with a massive creak to find none other than Tommy Gasbarro, the man she'd planned to marry on that very day. He'd opened his thick winter coat to reveal a suit jacket and a pair of slacks. He carried a beautiful bouquet in his gloved hand— all from the list of wedding flowers that Claire had named. Orchids. Roses. Lilies.

"Tommy..." Lola breathed as her eyes reached his. Her eyes trailed from his shoes back up to his face.

"Lola," he rasped as he stepped toward her, wrapping his arm around her waist and placing the tip of his nose against hers. "What are you doing in this big house alone?"

Lola laughed outright as her eyes filled with tears. "I think I just realized what I'm doing here in this big house alone."

"What's that?"

"Waiting for you to come and save me— yet again."

Tommy laughed and dropped his lips over hers, kissing her. "Go get dressed. Susan says there's something special for you in the upstairs closet."

"Those monsters planned this, didn't they?" Lola asked, shaking her head ominously.

Tommy didn't answer but instead waited for Lola downstairs as she shot up the staircase to find a gorgeous burgundy vintage dress, one that suited Lola's style perfectly. On the dress, someone had scribed a little note that said:

FOR THE BRIDE TO BE.

At first glance, Lola knew the handwriting belonged to Audrey.

Hurriedly, feeling the weight of her family at the Sunrise Cove and Tommy Gasbarro downstairs, Lola leaped into her gown, stepped into a pair of boots, and grabbed her coat. She lined her eyes with black eyeliner, painted her lips with bright-red lipstick, and touched up her dark eyebrows, a look that Audrey had called "sultry Italian beauty."

When Lola appeared at the top of the staircase, Tommy blinked up at her, captivated. Lola had half a mind to tease him, maybe call him her "prom date" or something like that. But luckily, she kept the thought to herself. She didn't want to ruin the magic of this moment.

"Between saying and doing is half a sea," Lola whispered when she reached him, echoing back the old Italian saying.

"Baby, we're going to do it. We'll do it all."

Tommy drove Lola back to the Sunrise Cove in his massive truck. On either side, enormous snow cliffs reached for the sky. All the while, Lola's and Tommy's hands were latched together in the center of the truck— a couple on the verge of something enormous, even if that something enormous wouldn't begin today.

As Tommy led Lola through the front door of the Sunrise Cove Bistro, the entirety of the Sheridan and Montgomery family burst out from either side of the Bistro in celebration. "Happy Engagement!" they cried joyously as "This Will Be Our Year" by The Zombies blared from speakers. Tear-filled, Lola lifted her chin to kiss Tommy as her heart beat like a teenager's. Perhaps she wasn't so different from Gail, Abby, and Rachel, after all.

"You tricked me!" Lola cried as she wrapped Audrey in a hug. "I was all alone in that big house, thinking the world had gone on without me."

"We had to do it," Audrey confessed. "It was the only way to really surprise you."

Susan, Amanda, and Christine hustled forward for hugs as well, each of them delivering their own words of love.

"You two were made for each other," Amanda began.

"I just love this guy, Lola. He's perfect for the family," Susan added.

"He dug the whole town out of a snowstorm, then he cleaned himself up as one of the most handsome on the island," Christine said, impressed. "No wonder he changed your opinion about marriage."

As Lola continued to celebrate with her extended family, sipping champagne and talking about the "true" wedding, which would probably come sometime during the summer, Lola glanced toward the far end of the Bistro, where Sunrise Cove guests sat eating dinner and sipping wine. Something curious caught Lola's attention— an oddly familiar couple seated across from one another were in conversation with a woman in her late twenties or early thirties.

The older woman in the couple sat facing away from Lola, but her motions were captivating. She talked expressively with her hands as she told a story that made both the young woman and the man burst into laughter.

With a funny jolt, Lola realized that the man at the table was none other than Hank, her Daddy Warbucks.

Which meant that...

It couldn't be.

Could it?

Lola hustled toward the far end of her party to get a better look. Sure enough, the beautiful Cora sat at a table with Hank and a woman who seemed to be his adult daughter. The three of them seemed to alternate between jokes and laughter, parading their way through a bottle of wine as another soft snow fluttered down outside. Lola's heart seized with wonder at the sight.

She felt she witnessed something incredible.

A woman who'd thought all was lost, taking the first steps toward hope.

A man who was open enough to let her take her time.

Lola turned back to watch Tommy in conversation with Scott, his soon-to-be brother-in-law. Scott smacked Tommy on the back as laughter erupted through him.

Tommy had never wanted this life. He'd never wanted a family. He'd never wanted comfort or to be in the same port for too long.

Yet here, at the Sunrise Cove, he'd found a home with Lola and the rest of her family.

Lola couldn't have written an ending better than this. And she knew so much of their story was still to come. All she had to do was lift her eyes to the horizon and have enough strength in her heart to dream and hope.

Epilogue

I n the days that followed, the island of Martha's Vineyard slowly recovered from the densest blizzard it had seen in fifty years. School was canceled for several days, resulting in a small population of snowmen cropping up across the Edgartown, Oak Bluffs, and West Tisbury communities. With Max on a little sleigh, Mia in Christine's little pouch, and the rest of the sisters and their daughters all bundled up, the Sheridan women walked through town, admiring the snowy scenery, grabbing baked goods from local cafés, and enjoying the magic of a slowed-laden island. The island would look like a completely different place in just five months, chaotic with summer vacationers and bright with hot sun.

On Wednesday morning, Lola received a phone call from one of the city-wide event organizers, Amelia, who asked if she might want to gather her theater troupe for "one last try" for the musical *Annie*. After that, Lola called each and every crew member to ask about their schedule. Each agreed to meet at three that afternoon for a final rehearsal before what would almost assuredly be a "rugged yet lovable" take on *Annie* that evening.

By seven, the auditorium was nearly filled with Vineyard residents, all hungry for local talent. At seven thirty, the curtains parted to exuberant applause. And by nine, Cora had already brought down the house with her miraculous musical numbers, so much so that the applause went on far too long and lingered into the next scene.

After Lola, Audrey, Amanda, Cora, Hank, and the rest of the crew stood out on stage and bowed low, Lola thanked the audience for honoring their community on the Vineyard and showing up when times got tough.

"We've been through quite a lot together," Lola said softly, her eyes glazing over as she looked out across three hundred Vineyard residents. "But we've proven that we're better together. I am so proud to be a part of this community and to call Martha's Vineyard my home. Thank you for welcoming us on stage tonight. Remember the words Annie says, which are words to live by. 'I don't need sunshine now to turn my skies to blue. I don't need anything but you.'"

Next in the Vineyard Series

Start Reading A Vineyard Bride

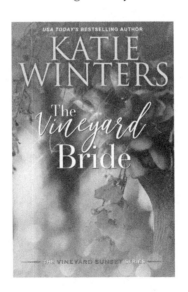

Other Books by Katie Winters

The Vineyard Sunset Series

Secrets of Mackinac Island Series

Sisters of Edgartown Series

A Katama Bay Series

A Mount Desert Island Series

A Nantucket Sunset Series